Oscar Fingal O'Flahertie Wills Wilde (16 October 1854 – 30 November 1900) was an Irish poet and playwright. After writing in different forms throughout the 1880s, he became one of London's most popular playwrights in the early 1890s. He is best remembered for his epigrams and plays, his novel The Picture of Dorian Gray, and the circumstances of his criminal conviction for homosexuality, imprisonment, and early death at age 46. Wilde's parents were successful Anglo-Irish intellectuals in Dublin. Their son became fluent in French and German early in life. At university, Wilde read Greats; he proved himself to be an outstanding classicist, first at Trinity College Dublin, then at Oxford. He became known for his involvement in the rising philosophy of aestheticism, led by two of his tutors, Walter Pater and John Ruskin. After university, Wilde moved to London into fashionable cultural and social circles. (Source: Wikipedia)

Literary works:
Ravenna (1878)
Poems (1881)
The Happy Prince and Other Stories (1888)
Lord Arthur Savile's Crime and Other Stories (1891)
A House of Pomegranates (1891)
Intentions (1891)
The Picture of Dorian Gray (1890)
The Soul of Man under Socialism (1891)
Lady Windermere's Fan (1892)
A Woman of No Importance (1893)
An Ideal Husband (1898)
The Importance of Being Earnest (1898)
De Profundis (1905)
The Ballad of Reading Gaol (1898)
The Portrait of Mr. W. H. (1889)

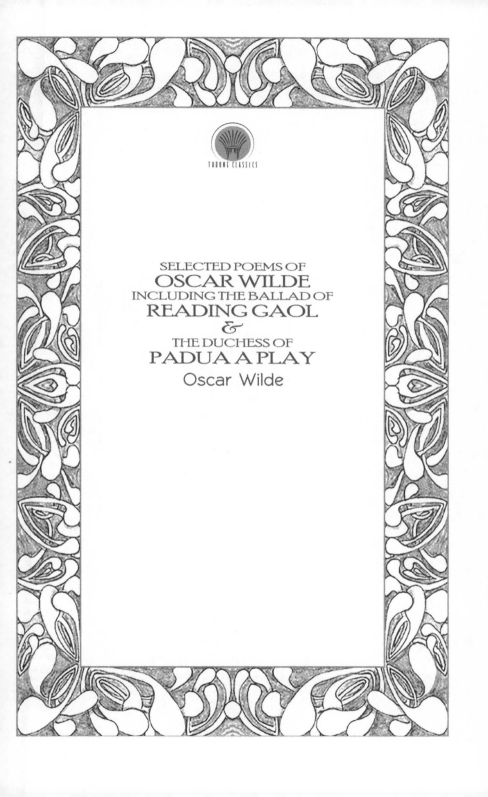

THRONE CLASSICS

SELECTED POEMS OF
OSCAR WILDE
INCLUDING THE BALLAD OF
READING GAOL
&
THE DUCHESS OF
PADUA A PLAY
Oscar Wilde

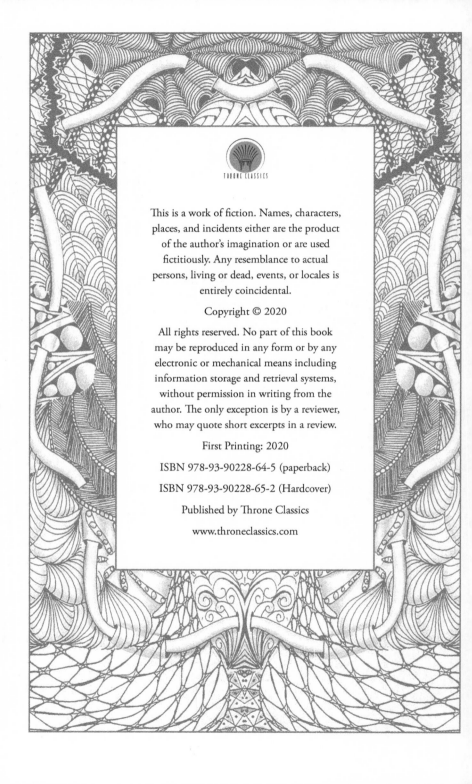

First Printing: 2020

ISBN 978-93-90228-64-5 (paperback)

ISBN 978-93-90228-65-2 (Hardcover)

Published by Throne Classics

www.throneclassics.com

Contents

SELECTED POEMS OF
OSCAR WILDE
INCLUDING THE BALLAD OF
READING GAOL
&
THE DUCHESS OF
PADUA A PLAY

SELECTED POEMS OF OSCAR WILDE INCLUDING THE BALLAD OF READING GAOL

PREFACE

It is thought that a selection from Oscar Wilde's early verses may be of interest to a large public at present familiar only with the always popular *Ballad of Reading Gaol,* also included in this volume. The poems were first collected by their author when he was twenty-sex years old, and though never, until recently, well received by the critics, have survived the test of NINE editions. Readers will be able to make for themselves the obvious and striking contrasts between these first and last phases of Oscar Wilde's literary activity. The intervening period was devoted almost entirely to dramas, prose, fiction, essays, and criticism.

ROBERT ROSS

Reform Club,

April 5, 1911.

NOTE

At the end of the complete text will be found a shorter version based on the original draft of the poem. This is included for the benefit of reciters and their audiences who have found the entire poem too long for declamation. I have tried to obviate a difficulty, without officiously exercising the ungrateful prerogatives of a literary executor, by falling back on a text which represents the author's first scheme for a poem—never intended of course for recitation.

ROBERT ROSS

IN MEMORIAM

C. T. W.

Sometimes trooper of

The Royal Horse Guards

Obiit H.M. Prison

Reading, Berkshire

July 7th, 1896

THE BALLAD OF READING GAOL

I

He did not wear his scarlet coat,
  For blood and wine are red,
And blood and wine were on his hands
  When they found him with the dead,
The poor dead woman whom he loved,
  And murdered in her bed.

He walked amongst the Trial Men
  In a suit of shabby grey;
A cricket cap was on his head,
  And his step seemed light and gay;
But I never saw a man who looked
  So wistfully at the day.

I never saw a man who looked
  With such a wistful eye
Upon that little tent of blue
  Which prisoners call the sky,
And at every drifting cloud that went

With sails of silver by.

I walked, with other souls in pain,
    Within another ring,
And was wondering if the man had done
    A great or little thing,
When a voice behind me whispered low,
    'That fellow's got to swing.'

Dear Christ! the very prison walls
    Suddenly seemed to reel,
And the sky above my head became
    Like a casque of scorching steel;
And, though I was a soul in pain,
    My pain I could not feel.

I only knew what hunted thought
    Quickened his step, and why
He looked upon the garish day
    With such a wistful eye;
The man had killed the thing he loved,
    And so he had to die.

Yet each man kills the thing he loves,

By each let this be heard,
Some do it with a bitter look,
    Some with a flattering word,
The coward does it with a kiss,
    The brave man with a sword!

Some kill their love when they are young,
    And some when they are old;
Some strangle with the hands of Lust,
    Some with the hands of Gold:
The kindest use a knife, because
    The dead so soon grow cold.

Some love too little, some too long,
    Some sell, and others buy;
Some do the deed with many tears,
    And some without a sigh:
For each man kills the thing he loves,
    Yet each man does not die.

He does not die a death of shame
    On a day of dark disgrace,
Nor have a noose about his neck,

Nor a cloth upon his face,

Nor drop feet foremost through the floor

    Into an empty space.

He does not sit with silent men

    Who watch him night and day;

Who watch him when he tries to weep,

    And when he tries to pray;

Who watch him lest himself should rob

    The prison of its prey.

He does not wake at dawn to see

    Dread figures throng his room,

The shivering Chaplain robed in white,

    The Sheriff stern with gloom,

And the Governor all in shiny black,

    With the yellow face of Doom.

He does not rise in piteous haste

    To put on convict-clothes,

While some coarse-mouthed Doctor gloats, and notes

    Each new and nerve-twitched pose,

Fingering a watch whose little ticks

    Are like horrible hammer-blows.

He does not know that sickening thirst
   That sands one's throat, before
The hangman with his gardener's gloves
   Slips through the padded door,
And binds one with three leathern thongs,
   That the throat may thirst no more.

He does not bend his head to hear
   The Burial Office read,
Nor, while the terror of his soul
   Tells him he is not dead,
Cross his own coffin, as he moves
   Into the hideous shed.

He does not stare upon the air
   Through a little roof of glass:
He does not pray with lips of clay
   For his agony to pass;
Nor feel upon his shuddering cheek
   The kiss of Caiaphas.

II

Six weeks our guardsman walked the yard,

In the suit of shabby grey:

His cricket cap was on his head,

    And his step seemed light and gay,

But I never saw a man who looked

    So wistfully at the day.

I never saw a man who looked

    With such a wistful eye

Upon that little tent of blue

    Which prisoners call the sky,

And at every wandering cloud that trailed

    Its ravelled fleeces by.

He did not wring his hands, as do

    Those witless men who dare

To try to rear the changeling Hope

    In the cave of black Despair:

He only looked upon the sun,

    And drank the morning air.

He did not wring his hands nor weep,

    Nor did he peek or pine,

But he drank the air as though it held

Some healthful anodyne;

With open mouth he drank the sun

   As though it had been wine!

And I and all the souls in pain,

   Who tramped the other ring,

Forgot if we ourselves had done

   A great or little thing,

And watched with gaze of dull amaze

   The man who had to swing.

And strange it was to see him pass

   With a step so light and gay,

And strange it was to see him look

   So wistfully at the day,

And strange it was to think that he

   Had such a debt to pay.

For oak and elm have pleasant leaves

   That in the springtime shoot:

But grim to see is the gallows-tree,

   With its adder-bitten root,

And, green or dry, a man must die

Before it bears its fruit!

The loftiest place is that seat of grace
  For which all worldlings try:
But who would stand in hempen band
  Upon a scaffold high,
And through a murderer's collar take
  His last look at the sky?

It is sweet to dance to violins
  When Love and Life are fair:
To dance to flutes, to dance to lutes
  Is delicate and rare:
But it is not sweet with nimble feet
  To dance upon the air!

So with curious eyes and sick surmise
  We watched him day by day,
And wondered if each one of us
  Would end the self-same way,
For none can tell to what red Hell
  His sightless soul may stray.

At last the dead man walked no more

Amongst the Trial Men,
And I knew that he was standing up
  In the black dock's dreadful pen,
And that never would I see his face
  In God's sweet world again.

Like two doomed ships that pass in storm
  We had crossed each other's way:
But we made no sign, we said no word,
  We had no word to say;
For we did not meet in the holy night,
  But in the shameful day.

A prison wall was round us both,
  Two outcast men we were:
The world had thrust us from its heart,
  And God from out His care:
And the iron gin that waits for Sin
  Had caught us in its snare.

III

In Debtors' Yard the stones are hard,
  And the dripping wall is high,

25

So it was there he took the air

    Beneath the leaden sky,

And by each side a Warder walked,

    For fear the man might die.

Or else he sat with those who watched

    His anguish night and day;

Who watched him when he rose to weep,

    And when he crouched to pray;

Who watched him lest himself should rob

    Their scaffold of its prey.

The Governor was strong upon

    The Regulations Act:

The Doctor said that Death was but

    A scientific fact:

And twice a day the Chaplain called,

    And left a little tract.

And twice a day he smoked his pipe,

    And drank his quart of beer:

His soul was resolute, and held

    No hiding-place for fear;

He often said that he was glad
   The hangman's hands were near.

But why he said so strange a thing
   No Warder dared to ask:
For he to whom a watcher's doom
   Is given as his task,
Must set a lock upon his lips,
   And make his face a mask.

Or else he might be moved, and try
   To comfort or console:
And what should Human Pity do
   Pent up in Murderers' Hole?
What word of grace in such a place
   Could help a brother's soul?

With slouch and swing around the ring
   We trod the Fools' Parade!
We did not care: we knew we were
   The Devil's Own Brigade:
And shaven head and feet of lead
   Make a merry masquerade.

We tore the tarry rope to shreds

    With blunt and bleeding nails;

We rubbed the doors, and scrubbed the floors,

    And cleaned the shining rails:

And, rank by rank, we soaped the plank,

    And clattered with the pails.

We sewed the sacks, we broke the stones,

    We turned the dusty drill:

We banged the tins, and bawled the hymns,

    And sweated on the mill:

But in the heart of every man

    Terror was lying still.

So still it lay that every day

    Crawled like a weed-clogged wave:

And we forgot the bitter lot

    That waits for fool and knave,

Till once, as we tramped in from work,

    We passed an open grave.

With yawning mouth the yellow hole

Gaped for a living thing;
The very mud cried out for blood
To the thirsty asphalte ring:
And we knew that ere one dawn grew fair
Some prisoner had to swing.

Right in we went, with soul intent
On Death and Dread and Doom:
The hangman, with his little bag,
Went shuffling through the gloom:
And each man trembled as he crept
Into his numbered tomb.

That night the empty corridors
Were full of forms of Fear,
And up and down the iron town
Stole feet we could not hear,
And through the bars that hide the stars
White faces seemed to peer.

He lay as one who lies and dreams
In a pleasant meadow-land,
The watchers watched him as he slept,

And could not understand

How one could sleep so sweet a sleep

With a hangman close at hand.

But there is no sleep when men must weep

Who never yet have wept:

So we—the fool, the fraud, the knave—

That endless vigil kept,

And through each brain on hands of pain

Another's terror crept.

Alas! it is a fearful thing

To feel another's guilt!

For, right within, the sword of Sin

Pierced to its poisoned hilt,

And as molten lead were the tears we shed

For the blood we had not spilt.

The Warders with their shoes of felt

Crept by each padlocked door,

And peeped and saw, with eyes of awe,

Grey figures on the floor,

And wondered why men knelt to pray

Who never prayed before.

All through the night we knelt and prayed,

    Mad mourners of a corse!

The troubled plumes of midnight were

    The plumes upon a hearse:

And bitter wine upon a sponge

    Was the savour of Remorse.

The grey cock crew, the red cock crew,

    But never came the day:

And crooked shapes of Terror crouched,

    In the corners where we lay:

And each evil sprite that walks by night

    Before us seemed to play.

They glided past, they glided fast,

    Like travellers through a mist:

They mocked the moon in a rigadoon

    Of delicate turn and twist,

And with formal pace and loathsome grace

    The phantoms kept their tryst.

With mop and mow, we saw them go,

Slim shadows hand in hand:

About, about, in ghostly rout

    They trod a saraband:

And the damned grotesques made arabesques,

    Like the wind upon the sand!

With the pirouettes of marionettes,

    They tripped on pointed tread:

But with flutes of Fear they filled the ear,

    As their grisly masque they led,

And loud they sang, and long they sang,

    For they sang to wake the dead.

'Oho!' they cried, 'The world is wide,

    But fettered limbs go lame!

And once, or twice, to throw the dice

    Is a gentlemanly game,

But he does not win who plays with Sin

    In the secret House of Shame.'

No things of air these antics were,

    That frolicked with such glee:

To men whose lives were held in gyves,

And whose feet might not go free,

Ah! wounds of Christ! they were living things,

Most terrible to see.

Around, around, they waltzed and wound;

Some wheeled in smirking pairs;

With the mincing step of a demirep

Some sidled up the stairs:

And with subtle sneer, and fawning leer,

Each helped us at our prayers.

The morning wind began to moan,

But still the night went on:

Through its giant loom the web of gloom

Crept till each thread was spun:

And, as we prayed, we grew afraid

Of the Justice of the Sun.

The moaning wind went wandering round

The weeping prison-wall:

Till like a wheel of turning steel

We felt the minutes crawl:

O moaning wind! what had we done

To have such a seneschal?

At last I saw the shadowed bars,

Like a lattice wrought in lead,

Move right across the whitewashed wall

That faced my three-plank bed,

And I knew that somewhere in the world

God's dreadful dawn was red.

At six o'clock we cleaned our cells,

At seven all was still,

But the sough and swing of a mighty wing

The prison seemed to fill,

For the Lord of Death with icy breath

Had entered in to kill.

He did not pass in purple pomp,

Nor ride a moon-white steed.

Three yards of cord and a sliding board

Are all the gallows' need:

So with rope of shame the Herald came

To do the secret deed.

We were as men who through a fen

Of filthy darkness grope:
We did not dare to breathe a prayer,
    Or to give our anguish scope:
Something was dead in each of us,
    And what was dead was Hope.

For Man's grim Justice goes its way,
    And will not swerve aside:
It slays the weak, it slays the strong,
    It has a deadly stride:
With iron heel it slays the strong,
    The monstrous parricide!

We waited for the stroke of eight:
    Each tongue was thick with thirst:
For the stroke of eight is the stroke of Fate
    That makes a man accursed,
And Fate will use a running noose
    For the best man and the worst.

We had no other thing to do,
    Save to wait for the sign to come:
So, like things of stone in a valley lone,

Quiet we sat and dumb:

But each man's heart beat thick and quick,

Like a madman on a drum!

With sudden shock the prison-clock

Smote on the shivering air,

And from all the gaol rose up a wail

Of impotent despair,

Like the sound that frightened marshes hear

From some leper in his lair.

And as one sees most fearful things

In the crystal of a dream,

We saw the greasy hempen rope

Hooked to the blackened beam,

And heard the prayer the hangman's snare

Strangled into a scream.

And all the woe that moved him so

That he gave that bitter cry,

And the wild regrets, and the bloody sweats,

None knew so well as I:

For he who lives more lives than one

More deaths than one must die.

IV

There is no chapel on the day
    On which they hang a man:
The Chaplain's heart is far too sick,
    Or his face is far too wan,
Or there is that written in his eyes
    Which none should look upon.

So they kept us close till nigh on noon,
    And then they rang the bell,
And the Warders with their jingling keys
    Opened each listening cell,
And down the iron stair we tramped,
    Each from his separate Hell.

Out into God's sweet air we went,
    But not in wonted way,
For this man's face was white with fear,
    And that man's face was grey,
And I never saw sad men who looked
    So wistfully at the day.

I never saw sad men who looked

   With such a wistful eye

Upon that little tent of blue

   We prisoners called the sky,

And at every careless cloud that passed

   In happy freedom by.

But there were those amongst us all

   Who walked with downcast head,

And knew that, had each got his due,

   They should have died instead:

He had but killed a thing that lived,

   Whilst they had killed the dead.

For he who sins a second time

   Wakes a dead soul to pain,

And draws it from its spotted shroud,

   And makes it bleed again,

And makes it bleed great gouts of blood,

   And makes it bleed in vain!

Like ape or clown, in monstrous garb

With crooked arrows starred,

Silently we went round and round

    The slippery asphalte yard;

Silently we went round and round,

    And no man spoke a word.

Silently we went round and round,

    And through each hollow mind

The Memory of dreadful things

    Rushed like a dreadful wind,

And Horror stalked before each man,

    And Terror crept behind.

The Warders strutted up and down,

    And kept their herd of brutes,

Their uniforms were spick and span,

    And they wore their Sunday suits,

But we knew the work they had been at,

    By the quicklime on their boots.

For where a grave had opened wide,

    There was no grave at all:

Only a stretch of mud and sand

By the hideous prison-wall,

And a little heap of burning lime,

That the man should have his pall.

For he has a pall, this wretched man,

Such as few men can claim:

Deep down below a prison-yard,

Naked for greater shame,

He lies, with fetters on each foot,

Wrapt in a sheet of flame!

And all the while the burning lime

Eats flesh and bone away,

It eats the brittle bone by night,

And the soft flesh by day,

It eats the flesh and bone by turns,

But it eats the heart alway.

For three long years they will not sow

Or root or seedling there:

For three long years the unblessed spot

Will sterile be and bare,

And look upon the wondering sky

With unreproachful stare.

They think a murderer's heart would taint
    Each simple seed they sow.
It is not true! God's kindly earth
    Is kindlier than men know,
And the red rose would but blow more red,
    The white rose whiter blow.

Out of his mouth a red, red rose!
    Out of his heart a white!
For who can say by what strange way,
    Christ brings His will to light,
Since the barren staff the pilgrim bore
    Bloomed in the great Pope's sight?

But neither milk-white rose nor red
    May bloom in prison-air;
The shard, the pebble, and the flint,
    Are what they give us there:
For flowers have been known to heal
    A common man's despair.

So never will wine-red rose or white,

Petal by petal, fall

On that stretch of mud and sand that lies

 By the hideous prison-wall,

To tell the men who tramp the yard

 That God's Son died for all.

Yet though the hideous prison-wall

 Still hems him round and round,

And a spirit may not walk by night

 That is with fetters bound,

And a spirit may but weep that lies

 In such unholy ground,

He is at peace—this wretched man—

 At peace, or will be soon:

There is no thing to make him mad,

 Nor does Terror walk at noon,

For the lampless Earth in which he lies

 Has neither Sun nor Moon.

They hanged him as a beast is hanged:

 They did not even toll

A requiem that might have brought

Rest to his startled soul,
But hurriedly they took him out,
    And hid him in a hole.

They stripped him of his canvas clothes,
    And gave him to the flies:
They mocked the swollen purple throat,
    And the stark and staring eyes:
And with laughter loud they heaped the shroud
    In which their convict lies.

The Chaplain would not kneel to pray
    By his dishonoured grave:
Nor mark it with that blessed Cross
    That Christ for sinners gave,
Because the man was one of those
    Whom Christ came down to save.

Yet all is well; he has but passed
    To Life's appointed bourne:
And alien tears will fill for him
    Pity's long-broken urn,
For his mourners will be outcast men,

And outcasts always mourn

V

I know not whether Laws be right,

Or whether Laws be wrong;

All that we know who lie in gaol

Is that the wall is strong;

And that each day is like a year,

A year whose days are long.

But this I know, that every Law

That men have made for Man,

Since first Man took his brother's life,

And the sad world began,

But straws the wheat and saves the chaff

With a most evil fan.

This too I know—and wise it were

If each could know the same—

That every prison that men build

Is built with bricks of shame,

And bound with bars lest Christ should see

How men their brothers maim.

With bars they blur the gracious moon,

 And blind the goodly sun:

And they do well to hide their Hell,

 For in it things are done

That Son of God nor son of Man

 Ever should look upon!

The vilest deeds like poison weeds,

 Bloom well in prison-air;

It is only what is good in Man

 That wastes and withers there:

Pale Anguish keeps the heavy gate,

 And the Warder is Despair.

For they starve the little frightened child

 Till it weeps both night and day:

And they scourge the weak, and flog the fool,

 And gibe the old and grey,

And some grow mad, and all grow bad,

 And none a word may say.

Each narrow cell in which we dwell

Is a foul and dark latrine,

And the fetid breath of living Death

Chokes up each grated screen,

And all, but Lust, is turned to dust

In Humanity's machine.

The brackish water that we drink

Creeps with a loathsome slime,

And the bitter bread they weigh in scales

Is full of chalk and lime,

And Sleep will not lie down, but walks

Wild-eyed, and cries to Time.

But though lean Hunger and green Thirst

Like asp with adder fight,

We have little care of prison fare,

For what chills and kills outright

Is that every stone one lifts by day

Becomes one's heart by night.

With midnight always in one's heart,

And twilight in one's cell,

We turn the crank, or tear the rope,

Each in his separate Hell,

And the silence is more awful far

   Than the sound of a brazen bell.

And never a human voice comes near

   To speak a gentle word:

And the eye that watches through the door

   Is pitiless and hard:

And by all forgot, we rot and rot,

   With soul and body marred.

And thus we rust Life's iron chain

   Degraded and alone:

And some men curse, and some men weep,

   And some men make no moan:

But God's eternal Laws are kind

   And break the heart of stone.

And every human heart that breaks,

   In prison-cell or yard,

Is as that broken box that gave

   Its treasure to the Lord,

And filled the unclean leper's house

With the scent of costliest nard.

Ah! happy they whose hearts can break

    And peace of pardon win!

How else may man make straight his plan

    And cleanse his soul from Sin?

How else but through a broken heart

    May Lord Christ enter in?

And he of the swollen purple throat,

    And the stark and staring eyes,

Waits for the holy hands that took

    The Thief to Paradise;

And a broken and a contrite heart

    The Lord will not despise.

The man in red who reads the Law

    Gave him three weeks of life,

Three little weeks in which to heal

    His soul of his soul's strife,

And cleanse from every blot of blood

    The hand that held the knife.

And with tears of blood he cleansed the hand,

The hand that held the steel:

For only blood can wipe out blood,

   And only tears can heal:

And the crimson stain that was of Cain

   Became Christ's snow-white seal.

VI

In Reading gaol by Reading town

   There is a pit of shame,

And in it lies a wretched man

   Eaten by teeth of flame,

In a burning winding-sheet he lies,

   And his grave has got no name.

And there, till Christ call forth the dead,

   In silence let him lie:

No need to waste the foolish tear,

   Or heave the windy sigh:

The man had killed the thing he loved,

   And so he had to die.

And all men kill the thing they love,

   By all let this be heard,

Some do it with a bitter look,

Some with a flattering word,

The coward does it with a kiss,

The brave man with a sword!

APPENDIX THE BALLAD OF READING GAOL

A VERSION BASED ON THE ORIGINAL DRAFT OF THE POEM

I

He did not wear his scarlet coat,
   For blood and wine are red,
And blood and wine were on his hands
   When they found him with the dead,
The poor dead woman whom he loved,
   And murdered in her bed.

He walked amongst the Trial Men
   In a suit of shabby grey;
A cricket cap was on his head,
   And his step seemed light and gay;
But I never saw a man who looked
   So wistfully at the day.

I never saw a man who looked
   With such a wistful eye
Upon that little tent of blue
   Which prisoners call the sky,

And at every drifting cloud that went

    With sails of silver by.

I walked, with other souls in pain,

    Within another ring,

And was wondering if the man had done

    A great or little thing,

When a voice behind me whispered low,

    'That fellow's got to swing.'

Dear Christ! the very prison walls

    Suddenly seemed to reel,

And the sky above my head became

    Like a casque of scorching steel;

And, though I was a soul in pain,

    My pain I could not feel.

I only knew what hunted thought

    Quickened his step, and why

He looked upon the garish day

    With such a wistful eye;

The man had killed the thing he loved,

    And so he had to die.

Yet each man kills the thing he loves,

   By each let this be heard,

Some do it with a bitter look,

   Some with a flattering word,

The coward does it with a kiss,

   The brave man with a sword!

Some kill their love when they are young,

   And some when they are old;

Some strangle with the hands of Lust,

   Some with the hands of Gold:

The kindest use a knife, because

   The dead so soon grow cold.

Some love too little, some too long,

   Some sell, and others buy;

Some do the deed with many tears,

   And some without a sigh:

For each man kills the thing he loves,

   Yet each man does not die.

He does not die a death of shame

On a day of dark disgrace,

Nor have a noose about his neck,

Nor a cloth upon his face,

Nor drop feet foremost through the floor

Into an empty space.

He does not wake at dawn to see

Dread figures throng his room,

The shivering Chaplain robed in white,

The Sheriff stern with gloom,

And the Governor all in shiny black,

With the yellow face of Doom.

He does not rise in piteous haste

To put on convict-clothes,

While some coarse-mouthed Doctor gloats, and notes

Each new and nerve-twitched pose,

Fingering a watch whose little ticks

Are like horrible hammer-blows.

He does not know that sickening thirst

That sands one's throat, before

The hangman with his gardener's gloves

Slips through the padded door,

And binds one with three leathern thongs,

   That the throat may thirst no more.

He does not bend his head to hear

   The Burial Office read,

Nor, while the terror of his soul

   Tells him he is not dead,

Cross his own coffin, as he moves

   Into the hideous shed.

He does not stare upon the air

   Through a little roof of glass:

He does not pray with lips of clay

   For his agony to pass;

Nor feel upon his shuddering cheek

   The kiss of Caiaphas.

II

Six weeks our guardsman walked the yard,

   In the suit of shabby grey:

His cricket cap was on his head,

   And his step seemed light and gay,

But I never saw a man who looked

So wistfully at the day.

He did not wring his hands nor weep,
    Nor did he peek or pine,
But he drank the air as though it held
    Some healthful anodyne;
With open mouth he drank the sun
    As though it had been wine!

And I and all the souls in pain,
    Who tramped the other ring,
Forgot if we ourselves had done
    A great or little thing,
And watched with gaze of dull amaze
    The man who had to swing.

So with curious eyes and sick surmise
    We watched him day by day,
And wondered if each one of us
    Would end the self-same way,
For none can tell to what red Hell
    His sightless soul may stray.

At last the dead man walked no more

Amongst the Trial Men,

And I knew that he was standing up

  In the black dock's dreadful pen,

And that never would I see his face

  In God's sweet world again.

Like two doomed ships that pass in storm

  We had crossed each other's way:

But we made no sign, we said no word,

  We had no word to say;

For we did not meet in the holy night,

  But in the shameful day.

A prison wall was round us both,

  Two outcast men we were:

The world had thrust us from its heart,

  And God from out His care:

And the iron gin that waits for Sin

  Had caught us in its snare.

III

In Debtors' Yard the stones are hard,

  And the dripping wall is high,

So it was there he took the air

   Beneath the leaden sky,

And by each side a Warder walked,

   For fear the man might die.

Or else he sat with those who watched

   His anguish night and day;

Who watched him when he rose to weep,

   And when he crouched to pray;

Who watched him lest himself should rob

   Their scaffold of its prey.

And twice a day he smoked his pipe,

   And drank his quart of beer:

His soul was resolute, and held

   No hiding-place for fear;

He often said that he was glad

   The hangman's hands were near.

But why he said so strange a thing

   No Warder dared to ask:

For he to whom a watcher's doom

   Is given as his task,

Must set a lock upon his lips,

    And make his face a mask.

With slouch and swing around the ring

    We trod the Fools' Parade!

We did not care: we knew we were

    The Devil's Own Brigade:

And shaven head and feet of lead

    Make a merry masquerade.

We tore the tarry rope to shreds

    With blunt and bleeding nails;

We rubbed the doors, and scrubbed the floors,

    And cleaned the shining rails:

And, rank by rank, we soaped the plank,

    And clattered with the pails.

We sewed the sacks, we broke the stones,

    We turned the dusty drill:

We banged the tins, and bawled the hymns,

    And sweated on the mill:

But in the heart of every man

    Terror was lying still.

So still it lay that every day

    Crawled like a weed-clogged wave:

And we forgot the bitter lot

    That waits for fool and knave,

Till once, as we tramped in from work,

    We passed an open grave.

Right in we went, with soul intent

    On Death and Dread and Doom:

The hangman, with his little bag,

    Went shuffling through the gloom:

And each man trembled as he crept

    Into his numbered tomb.

That night the empty corridors

    Were full of forms of Fear,

And up and down the iron town

    Stole feet we could not hear,

And through the bars that hide the stars

    White faces seemed to peer.

But there is no sleep when men must weep

Who never yet have wept:
So we—the fool, the fraud, the knave—
   That endless vigil kept,
And through each brain on hands of pain
   Another's terror crept.

Alas! it is a fearful thing
   To feel another's guilt!
For, right within, the sword of Sin
   Pierced to its poisoned hilt,
And as molten lead were the tears we shed
   For the blood we had not spilt.

The Warders with their shoes of felt
   Crept by each padlocked door,
And peeped and saw, with eyes of awe,
   Grey figures on the floor,
And wondered why men knelt to pray
   Who never prayed before.

The morning wind began to moan,
   But still the night went on:
Through its giant loom the web of gloom

Crept till each thread was spun:

And, as we prayed, we grew afraid

    Of the Justice of the Sun.

At last I saw the shadowed bars,

    Like a lattice wrought in lead,

Move right across the whitewashed wall

    That faced my three-plank bed,

And I knew that somewhere in the world

    God's dreadful dawn was red.

At six o'clock we cleaned our cells,

    At seven all was still,

But the sough and swing of a mighty wing

    The prison seemed to fill,

For the Lord of Death with icy breath

    Had entered in to kill.

He did not pass in purple pomp,

    Nor ride a moon-white steed.

Three yards of cord and a sliding board

    Are all the gallows' need:

So with rope of shame the Herald came

To do the secret deed.

We waited for the stroke of eight:

  Each tongue was thick with thirst:

For the stroke of eight is the stroke of Fate

  That makes a man accursed,

And Fate will use a running noose

  For the best man and the worst.

We had no other thing to do,

  Save to wait for the sign to come:

So, like things of stone in a valley lone,

  Quiet we sat and dumb:

But each man's heart beat thick and quick,

  Like a madman on a drum!

With sudden shock the prison-clock

  Smote on the shivering air,

And from all the gaol rose up a wail

  Of impotent despair,

Like the sound that frightened marshes hear

  From some leper in his lair.

And as one sees most fearful things

In the crystal of a dream,

We saw the greasy hempen rope

Hooked to the blackened beam,

And heard the prayer the hangman's snare

Strangled into a scream.

And all the woe that moved him so

That he gave that bitter cry,

And the wild regrets, and the bloody sweats,

None knew so well as I:

For he who lives more lives than one

More deaths than one must die.

IV

There is no chapel on the day

On which they hang a man:

The Chaplain's heart is far too sick,

Or his face is far too wan,

Or there is that written in his eyes

Which none should look upon.

So they kept us close till nigh on noon,

And then they rang the bell,

And the Warders with their jingling keys

    Opened each listening cell,

And down the iron stair we tramped,

    Each from his separate Hell.

Out into God's sweet air we went,

    But not in wonted way,

For this man's face was white with fear,

    And that man's face was grey,

And I never saw sad men who looked

    So wistfully at the day.

I never saw sad men who looked

    With such a wistful eye

Upon that little tent of blue

    We prisoners called the sky,

And at every careless cloud that passed

    In happy freedom by.

But there were those amongst us all

    Who walked with downcast head,

And knew that, had each got his due,

    They should have died instead:

He had but killed a thing that lived,

   Whilst they had killed the dead.

For he who sins a second time

   Wakes a dead soul to pain,

And draws it from its spotted shroud,

   And makes it bleed again,

And makes it bleed great gouts of blood,

   And makes it bleed in vain!

Like ape or clown, in monstrous garb

   With crooked arrows starred,

Silently we went round and round

   The slippery asphalte yard;

Silently we went round and round,

   And no man spoke a word.

Silently we went round and round,

   And through each hollow mind

The Memory of dreadful things

   Rushed like a dreadful wind,

And Horror stalked before each man,

   And Terror crept behind.

The Warders strutted up and down,
     And kept their herd of brutes,
Their uniforms were spick and span,
     And they wore their Sunday suits,
But we knew the work they had been at,
     By the quicklime on their boots.

For where a grave had opened wide,
     There was no grave at all:
Only a stretch of mud and sand
     By the hideous prison-wall,
And a little heap of burning lime,
     That the man should have his pall.

For he has a pall, this wretched man,
     Such as few men can claim:
Deep down below a prison-yard,
     Naked for greater shame,
He lies, with fetters on each foot,
     Wrapt in a sheet of flame!

For three long years they will not sow

Or root or seedling there:

For three long years the unblessed spot

Will sterile be and bare,

And look upon the wondering sky

With unreproachful stare.

They think a murderer's heart would taint

Each simple seed they sow.

It is not true! God's kindly earth

Is kindlier than men know,

And the red rose would but blow more red,

The white rose whiter blow.

Out of his mouth a red, red rose!

Out of his heart a white!

For who can say by what strange way,

Christ brings His will to light,

Since the barren staff the pilgrim bore

Bloomed in the great Pope's sight?

But neither milk-white rose nor red

May bloom in prison-air;

The shard, the pebble, and the flint,

Are what they give us there:

For flowers have been known to heal

    A common man's despair.

So never will wine-red rose or white,

    Petal by petal, fall

On that stretch of mud and sand that lies

    By the hideous prison-wall,

To tell the men who tramp the yard

    That God's Son died for all.

He is at peace—this wretched man—

    At peace, or will be soon:

There is no thing to make him mad,

    Nor does Terror walk at noon,

For the lampless Earth in which he lies

    Has neither Sun nor Moon.

The Chaplain would not kneel to pray

    By his dishonoured grave:

Nor mark it with that blessed Cross

    That Christ for sinners gave,

Because the man was one of those

Whom Christ came down to save.

Yet all is well; he has but passed

To Life's appointed bourne:

And alien tears will fill for him

Pity's long-broken urn,

For his mourners will be outcast men,

And outcasts always mourn.

POEMS

AVE IMPERATRIX

Set in this stormy Northern sea,
    Queen of these restless fields of tide,
England! what shall men say of thee,
    Before whose feet the worlds divide?

The earth, a brittle globe of glass,
    Lies in the hollow of thy hand,
And through its heart of crystal pass,
    Like shadows through a twilight land,

The spears of crimson-suited war,
    The long white-crested waves of fight,
And all the deadly fires which are
    The torches of the lords of Night.

The yellow leopards, strained and lean,
    The treacherous Russian knows so well,
With gaping blackened jaws are seen

Leap through the hail of screaming shell.

The strong sea-lion of England's wars

    Hath left his sapphire cave of sea,

To battle with the storm that mars

    The stars of England's chivalry.

The brazen-throated clarion blows

    Across the Pathan's reedy fen,

And the high steeps of Indian snows

    Shake to the tread of armèd men.

And many an Afghan chief, who lies

    Beneath his cool pomegranate-trees,

Clutches his sword in fierce surmise

    When on the mountain-side he sees

The fleet-foot Marri scout, who comes

    To tell how he hath heard afar

The measured roll of English drums

    Beat at the gates of Kandahar.

For southern wind and east wind meet

Where, girt and crowned by sword and fire,

England with bare and bloody feet

  Climbs the steep road of wide empire.

O lonely Himalayan height,

  Grey pillar of the Indian sky,

Where saw'st thou last in clanging flight

  Our wingèd dogs of Victory?

The almond-groves of Samarcand,

  Bokhara, where red lilies blow,

And Oxus, by whose yellow sand

  The grave white-turbaned merchants go:

And on from thence to Ispahan,

  The gilded garden of the sun,

Whence the long dusty caravan

  Brings cedar wood and vermilion;

And that dread city of Cabool

  Set at the mountain's scarpèd feet,

Whose marble tanks are ever full

  With water for the noonday heat:

Where through the narrow straight Bazaar

    A little maid Circassian

Is led, a present from the Czar

    Unto some old and bearded Khan,—

Here have our wild war-eagles flown,

    And flapped wide wings in fiery fight;

But the sad dove, that sits alone

    In England—she hath no delight.

In vain the laughing girl will lean

    To greet her love with love-lit eyes:

Down in some treacherous black ravine,

    Clutching his flag, the dead boy lies.

And many a moon and sun will see

    The lingering wistful children wait

To climb upon their father's knee;

    And in each house made desolate

Pale women who have lost their lord

    Will kiss the relics of the slain—

Some tarnished epaulette—some sword—
  Poor toys to soothe such anguished pain.

For not in quiet English fields
  Are these, our brothers, lain to rest,
Where we might deck their broken shields
  With all the flowers the dead love best.

For some are by the Delhi walls,
  And many in the Afghan land,
And many where the Ganges falls
  Through seven mouths of shifting sand.

And some in Russian waters lie,
  And others in the seas which are
The portals to the East, or by
  The wind-swept heights of Trafalgar.

O wandering graves! O restless sleep!
  O silence of the sunless day!
O still ravine! O stormy deep!
  Give up your prey! Give up your prey!

And thou whose wounds are never healed,

Whose weary race is never won,

O Cromwell's England! must thou yield

For every inch of ground a son?

Go! crown with thorns thy gold-crowned head,

Change thy glad song to song of pain;

Wind and wild wave have got thy dead,

And will not yield them back again.

Wave and wild wind and foreign shore

Possess the flower of English land—

Lips that thy lips shall kiss no more,

Hands that shall never clasp thy hand.

What profit now that we have bound

The whole round world with nets of gold,

If hidden in our heart is found

The care that groweth never old?

What profit that our galleys ride,

Pine-forest-like, on every main?

Ruin and wreck are at our side,

Grim warders of the House of Pain.

Where are the brave, the strong, the fleet?

  Where is our English chivalry?

Wild grasses are their burial-sheet,

  And sobbing waves their threnody.

O loved ones lying far away,

  What word of love can dead lips send!

O wasted dust! O senseless clay!

  Is this the end! is this the end!

Peace, peace! we wrong the noble dead

  To vex their solemn slumber so;

Though childless, and with thorn-crowned head,

  Up the steep road must England go,

Yet when this fiery web is spun,

  Her watchmen shall descry from far

The young Republic like a sun

  Rise from these crimson seas of war.

TO MY WIFE
WITH A COPY OF MY POEMS

I can write no stately proem

    As a prelude to my lay;

From a poet to a poem

    I would dare to say.

For if of these fallen petals

    One to you seem fair,

Love will waft it till it settles

    On your hair.

And when wind and winter harden

    All the loveless land,

It will whisper of the garden,

    You will understand.

MAGDALEN WALKS

[*After gaining the Berkeley Gold Medal for Greek at Trinity College, Dublin, in 1874, Oscar Wilde proceeded to Oxford, where he obtained a demyship at Magdalen College. He is the only real poet on the books of that institution.*]

The little white clouds are racing over the sky,

   And the fields are strewn with the gold of the flower of March,

   The daffodil breaks under foot, and the tasselled larch

Sways and swings as the thrush goes hurrying by.

A delicate odour is borne on the wings of the morning breeze,

   The odour of deep wet grass, and of brown new-furrowed earth,

   The birds are singing for joy of the Spring's glad birth,

Hopping from branch to branch on the rocking trees.

And all the woods are alive with the murmur and sound of Spring,

   And the rose-bud breaks into pink on the climbing briar,

   And the crocus-bed is a quivering moon of fire

Girdled round with the belt of an amethyst ring.

And the plane to the pine-tree is whispering some tale of love

   Till it rustles with laughter and tosses its mantle of green,

And the gloom of the wych-elm's hollow is lit with the iris sheen
Of the burnished rainbow throat and the silver breast of a dove.

See! the lark starts up from his bed in the meadow there,
  Breaking the gossamer threads and the nets of dew,
  And flashing adown the river, a flame of blue!
The kingfisher flies like an arrow, and wounds the air.

THEOCRITUS

A VILLANELLE

O singer of Persephone!
  In the dim meadows desolate
Dost thou remember Sicily?

Still through the ivy flits the bee
  Where Amaryllis lies in state;
O Singer of Persephone!

Simætha calls on Hecate
  And hears the wild dogs at the gate;
Dost thou remember Sicily?

Still by the light and laughing sea
  Poor Polypheme bemoans his fate;
O Singer of Persephone!

And still in boyish rivalry
  Young Daphnis challenges his mate;
Dost thou remember Sicily?

Slim Lacon keeps a goat for thee,

For thee the jocund shepherds wait;

O Singer of Persephone!

Dost thou remember Sicily?

SONNETS

GREECE

The sea was sapphire coloured, and the sky

Burned like a heated opal through the air;

   We hoisted sail; the wind was blowing fair

For the blue lands that to the eastward lie.

From the steep prow I marked with quickening eye

   Zakynthos, every olive grove and creek,

   Ithaca's cliff, Lycaon's snowy peak,

And all the flower-strewn hills of Arcady.

The flapping of the sail against the mast,

   The ripple of the water on the side,

   The ripple of girls' laughter at the stern,

The only sounds:—when 'gan the West to burn,

   And a red sun upon the seas to ride,

   I stood upon the soil of Greece at last!

KATAKOLO.

PORTIA

TO ELLEN TERRY

(Written at the Lyceum Theatre)

I marvel not Bassanio was so bold

    To peril all he had upon the lead,

    Or that proud Aragon bent low his head

Or that Morocco's fiery heart grew cold:

For in that gorgeous dress of beaten gold

    Which is more golden than the golden sun

    No woman Veronesé looked upon

Was half so fair as thou whom I behold.

Yet fairer when with wisdom as your shield

    The sober-suited lawyer's gown you donned,

And would not let the laws of Venice yield

    Antonio's heart to that accursèd Jew—

    O Portia! take my heart: it is thy due:

I think I will not quarrel with the Bond.

FABIEN DEI FRANCHI

TO MY FRIEND HENRY IRVING

The silent room, the heavy creeping shade,

    The dead that travel fast, the opening door,

    The murdered brother rising through the floor,

    The ghost's white fingers on thy shoulders laid,

And then the lonely duel in the glade,

    The broken swords, the stifled scream, the gore,

    Thy grand revengeful eyes when all is o'er,—

These things are well enough,—but thou wert made

    For more august creation! frenzied Lear

    Should at thy bidding wander on the heath

    With the shrill fool to mock him, Romeo

For thee should lure his love, and desperate fear

Pluck Richard's recreant dagger from its sheath—

    Thou trumpet set for Shakespeare's lips to blow!

PHÈDRE

TO SARAH BERNHARDT

How vain and dull this common world must seem

    To such a One as thou, who should'st have talked

At Florence with Mirandola, or walked

Through the cool olives of the Academe:

Thou should'st have gathered reeds from a green stream

    For Goat-foot Pan's shrill piping, and have played

    With the white girls in that Phæacian glade

Where grave Odysseus wakened from his dream.

Ah! surely once some urn of Attic clay

    Held thy wan dust, and thou hast come again

Back to this common world so dull and vain,

For thou wert weary of the sunless day,

The heavy fields of scentless asphodel,

The loveless lips with which men kiss in Hell.

SONNET

ON HEARING THE DIES IRÆ SUNG IN THE SISTINE CHAPEL

Nay, Lord, not thus! white lilies in the spring,

Sad olive-groves, or silver-breasted dove,

Teach me more clearly of Thy life and love

Than terrors of red flame and thundering.

The hillside vines dear memories of Thee bring:

A bird at evening flying to its nest

Tells me of One who had no place of rest:

I think it is of Thee the sparrows sing.

Come rather on some autumn afternoon,

When red and brown are burnished on the leaves,

And the fields echo to the gleaner's song,

Come when the splendid fulness of the moon

Looks down upon the rows of golden sheaves,

And reap Thy harvest: we have waited long.

AVE MARIA GRATIA PLENA

Was this His coming! I had hoped to see

   A scene of wondrous glory, as was told

   Of some great God who in a rain of gold

Broke open bars and fell on Danae:

Or a dread vision as when Semele

   Sickening for love and unappeased desire

   Prayed to see God's clear body, and the fire

Caught her brown limbs and slew her utterly:

With such glad dreams I sought this holy place,

   And now with wondering eyes and heart I stand

   Before this supreme mystery of Love:

Some kneeling girl with passionless pale face,

   An angel with a lily in his hand,

   And over both the white wings of a Dove.

FLORENCE.

LIBERTATIS SACRA FAMES

Albeit nurtured in democracy,

   And liking best that state republican

   Where every man is Kinglike and no man

Is crowned above his fellows, yet I see,

Spite of this modern fret for Liberty,

    Better the rule of One, whom all obey,

    Than to let clamorous demagogues betray

Our freedom with the kiss of anarchy.

Wherefore I love them not whose hands profane

    Plant the red flag upon the piled-up street

    For no right cause, beneath whose ignorant reign

Arts, Culture, Reverence, Honour, all things fade,

    Save Treason and the dagger of her trade,

    Or Murder with his silent bloody feet.

ROSES AND RUE

(To L. L.)

Could we dig up this long-buried treasure,

    Were it worth the pleasure,

We never could learn love's song,

    We are parted too long.

Could the passionate past that is fled

    Call back its dead,

Could we live it all over again,

    Were it worth the pain!

I remember we used to meet
By an ivied seat,
And you warbled each pretty word
With the air of a bird;

And your voice had a quaver in it,
Just like a linnet,
And shook, as the blackbird's throat
With its last big note;

And your eyes, they were green and grey
Like an April day,
But lit into amethyst
When I stooped and kissed;

And your mouth, it would never smile
For a long, long while,
Then it rippled all over with laughter
Five minutes after.

You were always afraid of a shower,
Just like a flower:

I remember you started and ran

    When the rain began.

I remember I never could catch you,

    For no one could match you,

You had wonderful, luminous, fleet,

    Little wings to your feet.

I remember your hair—did I tie it?

    For it always ran riot—

Like a tangled sunbeam of gold:

    These things are old.

I remember so well the room,

    And the lilac bloom

That beat at the dripping pane

    In the warm June rain;

And the colour of your gown,

    It was amber-brown,

And two yellow satin bows

    From your shoulders rose.

And the handkerchief of French lace

Which you held to your face—

Had a small tear left a stain?

  Or was it the rain?

On your hand as it waved adieu

  There were veins of blue;

In your voice as it said good-bye

  Was a petulant cry,

'You have only wasted your life.'

  (Ah, that was the knife!)

When I rushed through the garden gate

  It was all too late.

Could we live it over again,

  Were it worth the pain,

Could the passionate past that is fled

  Call back its dead!

Well, if my heart must break,

  Dear love, for your sake,

It will break in music, I know,

  Poets' hearts break so.

But strange that I was not told

That the brain can hold

In a tiny ivory cell

God's heaven and hell.

FROM 'THE GARDEN OF EROS'

[*In this poem the author laments the growth of materialism in the nineteenth century. He hails Keats and Shelley and some of the poets and artists who were his contemporaries, although his seniors, as the torch-bearers of the intellectual life. Among these are Swinburne, William Morris, Rossetti, and Brune-Jones.*]

Nay, when Keats died the Muses still had left

One silver voice to sing his threnody, [128]

But ah! too soon of it we were bereft

When on that riven night and stormy sea

Panthea claimed her singer as her own,

And slew the mouth that praised her; since which time we walk alone,

Save for that fiery heart, that morning star [129]

Of re-arisen England, whose clear eye

Saw from our tottering throne and waste of war

The grand Greek limbs of young Democracy

Rise mightily like Hesperus and bring

The great Republic! him at least thy love hath taught to sing,

And he hath been with thee at Thessaly,

  And seen white Atalanta fleet of foot

In passionless and fierce virginity

  Hunting the tuskèd boar, his honied lute

Hath pierced the cavern of the hollow hill,

And Venus laughs to know one knee will bow before her still.

And he hath kissed the lips of Proserpine,

  And sung the Galilæan's requiem,

That wounded forehead dashed with blood and wine

  He hath discrowned, the Ancient Gods in him

Have found their last, most ardent worshipper,

And the new Sign grows grey and dim before its conqueror.

Spirit of Beauty! tarry with us still,

  It is not quenched the torch of poesy,

The star that shook above the Eastern hill

  Holds unassailed its argent armoury

From all the gathering gloom and fretful fight—

O tarry with us still! for through the long and common night,

Morris, our sweet and simple Chaucer's child,

Dear heritor of Spenser's tuneful reed,

With soft and sylvan pipe has oft beguiled

The weary soul of man in troublous need,

And from the far and flowerless fields of ice

Has brought fair flowers to make an earthly paradise.

We know them all, Gudrun the strong men's bride,

Aslaug and Olafson we know them all,

How giant Grettir fought and Sigurd died,

And what enchantment held the king in thrall

When lonely Brynhild wrestled with the powers

That war against all passion, ah! how oft through summer hours,

Long listless summer hours when the noon

Being enamoured of a damask rose

Forgets to journey westward, till the moon

The pale usurper of its tribute grows

From a thin sickle to a silver shield

And chides its loitering car—how oft, in some cool grassy field

Far from the cricket-ground and noisy eight,

At Bagley, where the rustling bluebells come

Almost before the blackbird finds a mate

And overstay the swallow, and the hum

Of many murmuring bees flits through the leaves,

Have I lain poring on the dreamy tales his fancy weaves,

And through their unreal woes and mimic pain

   Wept for myself, and so was purified,

And in their simple mirth grew glad again;

   For as I sailed upon that pictured tide

The strength and splendour of the storm was mine

Without the storm's red ruin, for the singer is divine;

The little laugh of water falling down

   Is not so musical, the clammy gold

Close hoarded in the tiny waxen town

   Has less of sweetness in it, and the old

Half-withered reeds that waved in Arcady

Touched by his lips break forth again to fresher harmony.

Spirit of Beauty, tarry yet awhile!

   Although the cheating merchants of the mart

With iron roads profane our lovely isle,

   And break on whirling wheels the limbs of Art,

Ay! though the crowded factories beget

The blindworm Ignorance that slays the soul, O tarry yet!

For One at least there is,—He bears his name

   From Dante and the seraph Gabriel,—[136]

Whose double laurels burn with deathless flame

   To light thine altar; He [137] too loves thee well,

Who saw old Merlin lured in Vivien's snare,

And the white feet of angels coming down the golden stair,

Loves thee so well, that all the World for him

   A gorgeous-coloured vestiture must wear,

And Sorrow take a purple diadem,

   Or else be no more Sorrow, and Despair

Gild its own thorns, and Pain, like Adon, be

Even in anguish beautiful;—such is the empery

Which Painters hold, and such the heritage

   This gentle solemn Spirit doth possess,

Being a better mirror of his age

   In all his pity, love, and weariness,

Than those who can but copy common things,

And leave the Soul unpainted with its mighty questionings.

But they are few, and all romance has flown,

And men can prophesy about the sun,

And lecture on his arrows—how, alone,

   Through a waste void the soulless atoms run,

How from each tree its weeping nymph has fled,

And that no more 'mid English reeds a Naiad shows her head.

THE HARLOT'S HOUSE

We caught the tread of dancing feet,

We loitered down the moonlit street,

And stopped beneath the harlot's house.

Inside, above the din and fray,

We heard the loud musicians play

The 'Treues Liebes Herz' of Strauss.

Like strange mechanical grotesques,

Making fantastic arabesques,

The shadows raced across the blind.

We watched the ghostly dancers spin

To sound of horn and violin,

Like black leaves wheeling in the wind.

Like wire-pulled automatons,

Slim silhouetted skeletons

Went sidling through the slow quadrille,

Then took each other by the hand,

And danced a stately saraband;

Their laughter echoed thin and shrill.

Sometimes a clockwork puppet pressed

A phantom lover to her breast,

Sometimes they seemed to try to sing.

Sometimes a horrible marionette

Came out, and smoked its cigarette

Upon the steps like a live thing.

Then, turning to my love, I said,

'The dead are dancing with the dead,

The dust is whirling with the dust.'

But she—she heard the violin,

And left my side, and entered in:

Love passed into the house of lust.

Then suddenly the tune went false,

The dancers wearied of the waltz,

The shadows ceased to wheel and whirl.

And down the long and silent street,

The dawn, with silver-sandalled feet,

Crept like a frightened girl.

FROM 'THE BURDEN OF ITYS'

This English Thames is holier far than Rome,

   Those harebells like a sudden flush of sea

Breaking across the woodland, with the foam

   Of meadow-sweet and white anemone

To fleck their blue waves,—God is likelier there

Than hidden in that crystal-hearted star the pale monks bear!

Those violet-gleaming butterflies that take

   Yon creamy lily for their pavilion

Are monsignores, and where the rushes shake

   A lazy pike lies basking in the sun,

His eyes half shut,—he is some mitred old

Bishop in partibus! look at those gaudy scales all green and gold.

The wind the restless prisoner of the trees

   Does well for Palæstrina, one would say

The mighty master's hands were on the keys

   Of the Maria organ, which they play

When early on some sapphire Easter morn

In a high litter red as blood or sin the Pope is borne

From his dark House out to the Balcony

   Above the bronze gates and the crowded square,

Whose very fountains seem for ecstasy

   To toss their silver lances in the air,

And stretching out weak hands to East and West

In vain sends peace to peaceless lands, to restless nations rest.

Is not yon lingering orange after-glow

   That stays to vex the moon more fair than all

Rome's lordliest pageants! strange, a year ago

   I knelt before some crimson Cardinal

Who bare the Host across the Esquiline,

And now—those common poppies in the wheat seem twice as fine.

The blue-green beanfields yonder, tremulous

   With the last shower, sweeter perfume bring

Through this cool evening than the odorous

   Flame-jewelled censers the young deacons swing,

When the grey priest unlocks the curtained shrine,

And makes God's body from the common fruit of corn and vine.

Poor Fra Giovanni bawling at the Mass

   Were out of tune now, for a small brown bird

Sings overhead, and through the long cool grass

   I see that throbbing throat which once I heard

On starlit hills of flower-starred Arcady,

Once where the white and crescent sand of Salamis meets sea.

Sweet is the swallow twittering on the eaves

   At daybreak, when the mower whets his scythe,

And stock-doves murmur, and the milkmaid leaves

   Her little lonely bed, and carols blithe

To see the heavy-lowing cattle wait

Stretching their huge and dripping mouths across the farmyard gate.

And sweet the hops upon the Kentish leas,

   And sweet the wind that lifts the new-mown hay,

And sweet the fretful swarms of grumbling bees

   That round and round the linden blossoms play;

And sweet the heifer breathing in the stall,

And the green bursting figs that hang upon the red-brick wall,

And sweet to hear the cuckoo mock the spring

   While the last violet loiters by the well,

And sweet to hear the shepherd Daphnis sing

   The song of Linus through a sunny dell

Of warm Arcadia where the corn is gold

And the slight lithe-limbed reapers dance about the wattled fold.

* * * * *

It was a dream, the glade is tenantless,

   No soft Ionian laughter moves the air,

The Thames creeps on in sluggish leadenness,

   And from the copse left desolate and bare

Fled is young Bacchus with his revelry,

Yet still from Nuneham wood there comes that thrilling melody

So sad, that one might think a human heart

   Brake in each separate note, a quality

Which music sometimes has, being the Art

   Which is most nigh to tears and memory;

Poor mourning Philomel, what dost thou fear?

Thy sister doth not haunt these fields, Pandion is not here,

Here is no cruel Lord with murderous blade,

No woven web of bloody heraldries,

But mossy dells for roving comrades made,

   Warm valleys where the tired student lies

With half-shut book, and many a winding walk

Where rustic lovers stray at eve in happy simple talk.

The harmless rabbit gambols with its young

   Across the trampled towing-path, where late

A troop of laughing boys in jostling throng

   Cheered with their noisy cries the racing eight;

The gossamer, with ravelled silver threads,

Works at its little loom, and from the dusky red-eaved sheds

Of the lone Farm a flickering light shines out

   Where the swinked shepherd drives his bleating flock

Back to their wattled sheep-cotes, a faint shout

   Comes from some Oxford boat at Sandford lock,

And starts the moor-hen from the sedgy rill,

And the dim lengthening shadows flit like swallows up the hill.

The heron passes homeward to the mere,

   The blue mist creeps among the shivering trees,

Gold world by world the silent stars appear,

And like a blossom blown before the breeze

A white moon drifts across the shimmering sky,

Mute arbitress of all thy sad, thy rapturous threnody.

She does not heed thee, wherefore should she heed,

   She knows Endymion is not far away;

'Tis I, 'tis I, whose soul is as the reed

   Which has no message of its own to play,

So pipes another's bidding, it is I,

Drifting with every wind on the wide sea of misery.

Ah! the brown bird has ceased: one exquisite trill

   About the sombre woodland seems to cling

Dying in music, else the air is still,

   So still that one might hear the bat's small wing

Wander and wheel above the pines, or tell

Each tiny dew-drop dripping from the bluebell's brimming cell.

And far away across the lengthening wold,

   Across the willowy flats and thickets brown,

Magdalen's tall tower tipped with tremulous gold

   Marks the long High Street of the little town,

And warns me to return; I must not wait,

Hark! 't is the curfew booming from the bell at Christ Church gate.

FLOWER OF LOVE

Sweet, I blame you not, for mine the fault

was, had I not been made of common clay

I had climbed the higher heights unclimbed

yet, seen the fuller air, the larger day.

From the wildness of my wasted passion I had

struck a better, clearer song,

Lit some lighter light of freer freedom, battled

with some Hydra-headed wrong.

Had my lips been smitten into music by the

kisses that but made them bleed,

You had walked with Bice and the angels on

that verdant and enamelled mead.

I had trod the road which Dante treading saw

the suns of seven circles shine,

Ay! perchance had seen the heavens opening,

as they opened to the Florentine.

And the mighty nations would have crowned

me, who am crownless now and without name,

And some orient dawn had found me kneeling

on the threshold of the House of Fame.

I had sat within that marble circle where the

oldest bard is as the young,

And the pipe is ever dropping honey, and the

lyre's strings are ever strung.

Keats had lifted up his hymeneal curls from out

the poppy-seeded wine,

With ambrosial mouth had kissed my forehead,

clasped the hand of noble love in mine.

And at springtide, when the apple-blossoms

brush the burnished bosom of the dove,

Two young lovers lying in an orchard would

have read the story of our love;

Would have read the legend of my passion,

known the bitter secret of my heart,

Kissed as we have kissed, but never parted as

we two are fated now to part.

For the crimson flower of our life is eaten by

the cankerworm of truth,

And no hand can gather up the fallen withered

petals of the rose of youth.

Yet I am not sorry that I loved you—ah!

what else had I a boy to do,—

For the hungry teeth of time devour, and the

silent-footed years pursue.

Rudderless, we drift athwart a tempest, and

when once the storm of youth is past,

Without lyre, without lute or chorus, Death

the silent pilot comes at last.

And within the grave there is no pleasure,

for the blindworm battens on the root,

And Desire shudders into ashes, and the tree

of Passion bears no fruit.

Ah! what else had I to do but love you?

God's own mother was less dear to me,

And less dear the Cytheræan rising like an

argent lily from the sea.

I have made my choice, have lived my

poems, and, though youth is gone in wasted days,

I have found the lover's crown of myrtle better

than the poet's crown of bays.

FOOTNOTES

[128] Shelley.

[129] Swinburne.

[136] Rossetti.

[137] Burne-Jones.

THE DUCHESS OF PADUA: A PLAY

THE PERSONS OF THE PLAY

Simone Gesso, Duke of Padua

Beatrice, his Wife

Andreas Pollajuolo, Cardinal of Padua

Maffio Petrucci, Jeppo Vitellozzo, Taddeo Bardi } Gentlemen of the Duke's Household

Guido Ferranti, a Young Man

Ascanio Cristofano, his Friend

Count Moranzone, an Old Man

Bernardo Cavalcanti, Lord Justice of Padua

Hugo, the Headsman

Lucy, a Tire woman

Servants, Citizens, Soldiers, Monks, Falconers with their hawks and dogs, etc.

PLACE: *Padua*

TIME: *The latter half of the Sixteenth Century*

THE SCENES OF THE PLAY

Act I.	The Market Place of Padua (25 minutes).
Act II.	Room in the Duke's Palace (36 minutes).
Act III.	Corridor in the Duke's Palace (29 minutes).
Act IV.	The Hall of Justice (31 minutes).
Act V.	The Dungeon (25 minutes).

Style of Architecture: Italian, Gothic and Romanesque.

ACT I

SCENE

The Market Place of Padua at noon; in the background is the great Cathedral of Padua; the architecture is Romanesque, and wrought in black and white marbles; a flight of marble steps leads up to the Cathedral door; at the foot of the steps are two large stone lions; the houses on each side of the stage have coloured awnings from their windows, and are flanked by stone arcades; on the right of the stage is the public fountain, with a triton in green bronze blowing from a conch; around the fountain is a stone seat; the bell of the Cathedral is ringing, and the citizens, men, women and children, are passing into the Cathedral.

[Enter Guido Ferranti and Ascanio Cristofano.]

Now by my life, Guido, I will go no farther; for if I walk another step I will have no life left to swear by; this wild-goose errand of yours!

[Sits down on the step of the fountain.]

Guido

I think it must be here. [Goes up to passer-by and doffs his cap.] Pray, sir, is this the market place, and that the church of Santa Croce? [Citizen bows.] I thank you, sir.

Ascanio

Well?

Guido

Ay! it is here.

Ascanio

I would it were somewhere else, for I see no wine-shop.

Guido

[Taking a letter from his pocket and reading it.] 'The hour noon;

the city, Padua; the place, the market; and the day, Saint Philip's
Day.'

Ascanio

And what of the man, how shall we know him?

Guido [reading still]

'I will wear a violet cloak with a silver falcon broidered on the
shoulder.' A brave attire, Ascanio.

Ascanio

I'd sooner have my leathern jerkin. And you think he will tell you
of your father?

Guido

Why, yes! It is a month ago now, you remember; I was in the
vineyard, just at the corner nearest the road, where the goats used to
get in, a man rode up and asked me was my name Guido, and gave
me this letter, signed 'Your Father's Friend,' bidding me be here to-
day if I would know the secret of my birth, and telling me how to
recognise the writer! I had always thought old Pedro was my uncle,
but he told me that he was not, but that I had been left a child in
his charge by some one he had never since seen.

Ascanio

And you don't know who your father is?

Guido

No.

Ascanio

No recollection of him even?

Guido

None, Ascanio, none.

Ascanio [laughing]

Then he could never have boxed your ears so often as my father did mine.

Guido [smiling]

I am sure you never deserved it.

Ascanio

Never; and that made it worse. I hadn't the consciousness of guilt to buoy me up. What hour did you say he fixed?

Guido

Noon.

[*Clock in the Cathedral strikes.*]

Ascanio

It is that now, and your man has not come. I don't believe in him, Guido. I think it is some wench who has set her eye at you; and, as I have followed you from Perugia to Padua, I swear you shall follow me to the nearest tavern. [Rises.] By the great gods of eating, Guido, I am as hungry as a widow is for a husband, as tired as a young maid is of good advice, and as dry as a monk's sermon. Come, Guido, you stand there looking at nothing, like the fool who tried to look into his own mind; your man will not come.

Guido

Well, I suppose you are right. Ah! [Just as he is leaving the stage with Ascanio, enter Lord Moranzone in a violet cloak, with a silver falcon broidered on the shoulder; he passes across to the Cathedral, and just as he is going in Guido runs up and touches him.]

Moranzone

Guido Ferranti, thou hast come in time.

Guido

What! Does my father live?

Moranzone

Ay! lives in thee.

Thou art the same in mould and lineament,

Carriage and form, and outward semblances;

I trust thou art in noble mind the same.

Guido

Oh, tell me of my father; I have lived

But for this moment.

Moranzone

We must be alone.

Guido

This is my dearest friend, who out of love

Has followed me to Padua; as two brothers,

There is no secret which we do not share.

Moranzone

There is one secret which ye shall not share;

Bid him go hence.

Guido [to Ascanio]

Come back within the hour.

He does not know that nothing in this world

Can dim the perfect mirror of our love.

Within the hour come.

Ascanio

Speak not to him,

There is a dreadful terror in his look.

Guido [laughing]

Nay, nay, I doubt not that he has come to tell

That I am some great Lord of Italy,

And we will have long days of joy together.

Within the hour, dear Ascanio.

[Exit Ascanio.]

Now tell me of my father? [Sits down on a stone seat.]

Stood he tall?

I warrant he looked tall upon his horse.

His hair was black? or perhaps a reddish gold,

Like a red fire of gold? Was his voice low?

The very bravest men have voices sometimes

Full of low music; or a clarion was it

That brake with terror all his enemies?

Did he ride singly? or with many squires

And valiant gentlemen to serve his state?

For oftentimes methinks I feel my veins

Beat with the blood of kings. Was he a king?

Moranzone

Ay, of all men he was the kingliest.

Guido [proudly]

Then when you saw my noble father last

He was set high above the heads of men?

Moranzone

Ay, he was high above the heads of men,

[Walks over to Guido and puts his hand upon his shoulder.]

On a red scaffold, with a butcher's block

Set for his neck.

Guido [leaping up]

What dreadful man art thou,

That like a raven, or the midnight owl,

Com'st with this awful message from the grave?

Moranzone

I am known here as the Count Moranzone,

Lord of a barren castle on a rock,

With a few acres of unkindly land

And six not thrifty servants. But I was one

Of Parma's noblest princes; more than that,

I was your father's friend.

Guido [clasping his hand]

Tell me of him.

Moranzone

You are the son of that great Duke Lorenzo,

He was the Prince of Parma, and the Duke

Of all the fair domains of Lombardy

Down to the gates of Florence; nay, Florence even

Was wont to pay him tribute—

Guido

Come to his death.

Moranzone

You will hear that soon enough. Being at war—

O noble lion of war, that would not suffer

Injustice done in Italy!—he led

The very flower of chivalry against

That foul adulterous Lord of Rimini,

Giovanni Malatesta—whom God curse!

And was by him in treacherous ambush taken,

And like a villain, or a low-born knave,

Was by him on the public scaffold murdered.

Guido [clutching his dagger]

Doth Malatesta live?

Moranzone

No, he is dead.

Guido

Did you say dead? O too swift runner, Death,

Couldst thou not wait for me a little space,

And I had done thy bidding!

Moranzone [clutching his wrist]

Thou canst do it!

The man who sold thy father is alive.

Guido

Sold! was my father sold?

Moranzone

Ay! trafficked for,

Like a vile chattel, for a price betrayed,

Bartered and bargained for in privy market

By one whom he had held his perfect friend,

One he had trusted, one he had well loved,

One whom by ties of kindness he had bound—

Guido

And he lives

Who sold my father?

Moranzone

I will bring you to him.

Guido

So, Judas, thou art living! well, I will make

This world thy field of blood, so buy it straight-way,

For thou must hang there.

Moranzone

Judas said you, boy?

Yes, Judas in his treachery, but still

He was more wise than Judas was, and held

Those thirty silver pieces not enough.

Guido

What got he for my father's blood?

Moranzone

What got he?

Why cities, fiefs, and principalities,

Vineyards, and lands.

Guido

Of which he shall but keep

Six feet of ground to rot in. Where is he,

This damned villain, this foul devil? where?

Show me the man, and come he cased in steel,

In complete panoply and pride of war,

Ay, guarded by a thousand men-at-arms,

Yet I shall reach him through their spears, and feel

The last black drop of blood from his black heart

Crawl down my blade. Show me the man, I say,

And I will kill him.

Moranzone [coldly]

Fool, what revenge is there?

Death is the common heritage of all,

And death comes best when it comes suddenly.

                      [*Goes up close to* Guido.]

Your father was betrayed, there is your cue;

For you shall sell the seller in his turn.

I will make you of his household, you shall sit

At the same board with him, eat of his bread—

Guido

O bitter bread!

Moranzone

Thy palate is too nice,

Revenge will make it sweet. Thou shalt o' nights

Pledge him in wine, drink from his cup, and be

123

His intimate, so he will fawn on thee,

Love thee, and trust thee in all secret things.

If he bid thee be merry thou must laugh,

And if it be his humour to be sad

Thou shalt don sables. Then when the time is ripe—

[Guido *clutches his sword.*]

Nay, nay, I trust thee not; your hot young blood,

Undisciplined nature, and too violent rage

Will never tarry for this great revenge,

But wreck itself on passion.

Guido

Thou knowest me not.

Tell me the man, and I in everything

Will do thy bidding.

Moranzone

Well, when the time is ripe,

The victim trusting and the occasion sure,

I will by sudden secret messenger

Send thee a sign.

Guido

How shall I kill him, tell me?

Moranzone

That night thou shalt creep into his private chamber;

But if he sleep see that thou wake him first,

And hold thy hand upon his throat, ay! that way,

Then having told him of what blood thou art,

Sprung from what father, and for what revenge,

Bid him to pray for mercy; when he prays,

Bid him to set a price upon his life,

And when he strips himself of all his gold

Tell him thou needest not gold, and hast not mercy,

And do thy business straight away. Swear to me

Thou wilt not kill him till I bid thee do it,

Or else I go to mine own house, and leave

Thee ignorant, and thy father unavenged.

Guido

Now by my father's sword—

Moranzone

The common hangman

Brake that in sunder in the public square.

Guido

Then by my father's grave—

Moranzone

What grave? what grave?

Your noble father lieth in no grave,

I saw his dust strewn on the air, his ashes

Whirled through the windy streets like common straws

To plague a beggar's eyesight, and his head,

That gentle head, set on the prison spike,

For the vile rabble in their insolence

To shoot their tongues at.

Guido

Was it so indeed?

Then by my father's spotless memory,

And by the shameful manner of his death,

And by the base betrayal by his friend,

For these at least remain, by these I swear

I will not lay my hand upon his life

Until you bid me, then—God help his soul,

For he shall die as never dog died yet.

And now, the sign, what is it?

Moranzone

This dagger, boy;

It was your father's.

Guido

Oh, let me look at it!

I do remember now my reputed uncle,

That good old husbandman I left at home,

Told me a cloak wrapped round me when a babe

Bare too such yellow leopards wrought in gold;

I like them best in steel, as they are here,

They suit my purpose better. Tell me, sir,

Have you no message from my father to me?

Moranzone

> Poor boy, you never saw that noble father,
>
> For when by his false friend he had been sold,
>
> Alone of all his gentlemen I escaped
>
> To bear the news to Parma to the Duchess.

Guido

> Speak to me of my mother.

Moranzone

> When thy mother
>
> Heard my black news, she fell into a swoon,
>
> And, being with untimely travail seized—
>
> Bare thee into the world before thy time,
>
> And then her soul went heavenward, to wait
>
> Thy father, at the gates of Paradise.

Guido

> A mother dead, a father sold and bartered!
>
> I seem to stand on some beleaguered wall,
>
> And messenger comes after messenger
>
> With a new tale of terror; give me breath,
>
> Mine ears are tired.

Moranzone

> When thy mother died,
>
> Fearing our enemies, I gave it out
>
> Thou wert dead also, and then privily

Conveyed thee to an ancient servitor,

Who by Perugia lived; the rest thou knowest.

Guido

Saw you my father afterwards?

Moranzone

Ay! once;

In mean attire, like a vineyard dresser,

I stole to Rimini.

Guido [taking his hand]

O generous heart!

Moranzone

One can buy everything in Rimini,

And so I bought the gaolers! when your father

Heard that a man child had been born to him,

His noble face lit up beneath his helm

Like a great fire seen far out at sea,

And taking my two hands, he bade me, Guido,

To rear you worthy of him; so I have reared you

To revenge his death upon the friend who sold him.

Guido

Thou hast done well; I for my father thank thee.

And now his name?

Moranzone

How you remind me of him,

You have each gesture that your father had.

Guido

> The traitor's name?

Moranzone

> Thou wilt hear that anon;
>
> The Duke and other nobles at the Court
>
> Are coming hither.

Guido

> What of that? his name?

Moranzone

> Do they not seem a valiant company
>
> Of honourable, honest gentlemen?

Guido

> His name, milord?

[Enter the Duke of Padua with Count Bardi, Maffio, Petrucci, and other gentlemen of his Court.]

Moranzone [quickly]

> The man to whom I kneel
>
> Is he who sold your father! mark me well.

Guido [clutches hit dagger]

> The Duke!

Moranzone

> Leave off that fingering of thy knife.
>
> Hast thou so soon forgotten? [Kneels to the Duke.]
>
> My noble Lord.

Duke

> Welcome, Count Moranzone; 'tis some time

Since we have seen you here in Padua.

We hunted near your castle yesterday—

Call you it castle? that bleak house of yours

Wherein you sit a-mumbling o'er your beads,

Telling your vices like a good old man.

[*Catches sight of* Guido *and starts back.*]

Who is that?

Moranzone

My sister's son, your Grace,

Who being now of age to carry arms,

Would for a season tarry at your Court

Duke [still looking at Guido]

What is his name?

Moranzone

Guido Ferranti, sir.

Duke

His city?

Moranzone

He is Mantuan by birth.

Duke [advancing towards Guido]

You have the eyes of one I used to know,

But he died childless. Are you honest, boy?

Then be not spendthrift of your honesty,

But keep it to yourself; in Padua

Men think that honesty is ostentatious, so

130

It is not of the fashion. Look at these lords.

Count Bardi [aside]

> Here is some bitter arrow for us, sure.

Duke

> Why, every man among them has his price,
>
> Although, to do them justice, some of them
>
> Are quite expensive.

Count Bardi [aside]

> There it comes indeed.

Duke

> So be not honest; eccentricity
>
> Is not a thing should ever be encouraged,
>
> Although, in this dull stupid age of ours,
>
> The most eccentric thing a man can do
>
> Is to have brains, then the mob mocks at him;
>
> And for the mob, despise it as I do,
>
> I hold its bubble praise and windy favours
>
> In such account, that popularity
>
> Is the one insult I have never suffered.

Maffio [aside]

> He has enough of hate, if he needs that.

Duke

> Have prudence; in your dealings with the world
>
> Be not too hasty; act on the second thought,
>
> First impulses are generally good.

Guido [aside]

Surely a toad sits on his lips, and spills its venom there.

Duke

See thou hast enemies,

Else will the world think very little of thee;

It is its test of power; yet see thou show'st

A smiling mask of friendship to all men,

Until thou hast them safely in thy grip,

Then thou canst crush them.

Guido [aside]

O wise philosopher!

That for thyself dost dig so deep a grave.

Moranzone [to him]

Dost thou mark his words?

Guido

Oh, be thou sure I do.

Duke

And be not over-scrupulous; clean hands

With nothing in them make a sorry show.

If you would have the lion's share of life

You must wear the fox's skin. Oh, it will fit you;

It is a coat which fitteth every man.

Guido

Your Grace, I shall remember.

Duke

That is well, boy, well.

I would not have about me shallow fools,

Who with mean scruples weigh the gold of life,

And faltering, paltering, end by failure; failure,

The only crime which I have not committed:

I would have men about me. As for conscience,

Conscience is but the name which cowardice

Fleeing from battle scrawls upon its shield.

You understand me, boy?

Guido

I do, your Grace,

And will in all things carry out the creed

Which you have taught me.

Maffio

I never heard your Grace

So much in the vein for preaching; let the Cardinal

Look to his laurels, sir.

Duke

The Cardinal!

Men follow my creed, and they gabble his.

I do not think much of the Cardinal;

Although he is a holy churchman, and

I quite admit his dulness. Well, sir, from now

We count you of our household

[*He holds out his hand for* Guido *to kiss.* Guido *starts back in horror, but at a gesture from* Count Moranzone, *kneels and kisses it.*]

> We will see
>
> That you are furnished with such equipage
>
> As doth befit your honour and our state.

Guido

> I thank your Grace most heartily.

Duke

> Tell me again
>
> What is your name?

Guido

> Guido Ferranti, sir.

Duke

> And you are Mantuan? Look to your wives, my lords,
>
> When such a gallant comes to Padua.
>
> Thou dost well to laugh, Count Bardi; I have noted
>
> How merry is that husband by whose hearth
>
> Sits an uncomely wife.

Maffio

> May it please your Grace,
>
> The wives of Padua are above suspicion.

Duke

> What, are they so ill-favoured! Let us go,
>
> This Cardinal detains our pious Duchess;
>
> His sermon and his beard want cutting both:

Will you come with us, sir, and hear a text

From holy Jerome?

Moranzone [bowing]

My liege, there are some matters—

Duke [interrupting]

Thou need'st make no excuse for missing mass.

Come, gentlemen.

[*Exit with his suite into Cathedral.*]

Guido [after a pause]

So the Duke sold my father;

I kissed his hand.

Moranzone

Thou shalt do that many times.

Guido

Must it be so?

Moranzone

Ay! thou hast sworn an oath.

Guido

That oath shall make me marble.

Moranzone

Farewell, boy,

Thou wilt not see me till the time is ripe.

Guido

I pray thou comest quickly.

Moranzone

I will come

When it is time; be ready.

Guido

Fear me not.

Moranzone

Here is your friend; see that you banish him

Both from your heart and Padua.

Guido

From Padua,

Not from my heart.

Moranzone

Nay, from thy heart as well,

I will not leave thee till I see thee do it.

Guido

Can I have no friend?

Moranzone

Revenge shall be thy friend;

Thou need'st no other.

Guido

Well, then be it so.

[*Enter* Ascanio Cristofano.]

Ascanio

Come, Guido, I have been beforehand with you in everything, for I have drunk a flagon of wine, eaten a pasty, and kissed the maid who served it. Why, you look as melancholy as a schoolboy who cannot buy apples, or a politician who cannot sell his vote. What news, Guido, what news?

Guido

Why, that we two must part, Ascanio.

Ascanio

That would be news indeed, but it is not true.

Guido

Too true it is, you must get hence, Ascanio,

And never look upon my face again.

Ascanio

No, no; indeed you do not know me, Guido;

'Tis true I am a common yeoman's son,

Nor versed in fashions of much courtesy;

But, if you are nobly born, cannot I be

Your serving man? I will tend you with more love

Than any hired servant.

Guido [clasping his hand]

Ascanio!

[*Sees* Moranzone *looking at him and drops* Ascanio's *hand.*]

It cannot be.

Ascanio

What, is it so with you?

I thought the friendship of the antique world

Was not yet dead, but that the Roman type

Might even in this poor and common age

Find counterparts of love; then by this love

Which beats between us like a summer sea,

Whatever lot has fallen to your hand

May I not share it?

Guido

Share it?

Ascanio

Ay!

Guido

No, no.

Ascanio

Have you then come to some inheritance

Of lordly castle, or of stored-up gold?

Guido [bitterly]

Ay! I have come to my inheritance.

O bloody legacy! and O murderous dole!

Which, like the thrifty miser, must I hoard,

And to my own self keep; and so, I pray you,

Let us part here.

Ascanio

What, shall we never more

Sit hand in hand, as we were wont to sit,

Over some book of ancient chivalry

Stealing a truant holiday from school,

Follow the huntsmen through the autumn woods,

And watch the falcons burst their tasselled jesses,

When the hare breaks from covert.

Guido

Never more.

Ascanio

Must I go hence without a word of love?

Guido

You must go hence, and may love go with you.

Ascanio

You are unknightly, and ungenerous.

Guido

Unknightly and ungenerous if you will.

Why should we waste more words about the matter

Let us part now.

Ascanio

Have you no message, Guido?

Guido

None; my whole past was but a schoolboy's dream;

To-day my life begins. Farewell.

Ascanio

Farewell [exit slowly.]

Guido

Now are you satisfied? Have you not seen

My dearest friend, and my most loved companion,

Thrust from me like a common kitchen knave!

Oh, that I did it! Are you not satisfied?

Moranzone

Ay! I am satisfied. Now I go hence,

Do not forget the sign, your father's dagger,

And do the business when I send it to you.

Guido

Be sure I shall. [Exit Lord Moranzone.]

Guido

O thou eternal heaven!

If there is aught of nature in my soul,

Of gentle pity, or fond kindliness,

Wither it up, blast it, bring it to nothing,

Or if thou wilt not, then will I myself

Cut pity with a sharp knife from my heart

And strangle mercy in her sleep at night

Lest she speak to me. Vengeance there I have it.

Be thou my comrade and my bedfellow,

Sit by my side, ride to the chase with me,

When I am weary sing me pretty songs,

When I am light o' heart, make jest with me,

And when I dream, whisper into my ear

The dreadful secret of a father's murder—

Did I say murder? [Draws his dagger.]

Listen, thou terrible God!

Thou God that punishest all broken oaths,

And bid some angel write this oath in fire,

That from this hour, till my dear father's murder

In blood I have revenged, I do forswear

The noble ties of honourable friendship,

The noble joys of dear companionship,

Affection's bonds, and loyal gratitude,

Ay, more, from this same hour I do forswear

All love of women, and the barren thing

Which men call beauty—

[*The organ peals in the Cathedral, and under a canopy of cloth of silver tissue, borne by four pages in scarlet, the* Duchess of Padua *comes down the steps; as she passes across their eyes meet for a moment, and as she leaves the stage she looks back at* Guido, *and the dagger falls from his hand.*]

Oh! who is that?

A Citizen

The Duchess of Padua!

END OF ACT I.

ACT II

SCENE

A state room in the Ducal Palace, hung with tapestries representing the Masque of Venus; a large door in the centre opens into a corridor of red marble, through which one can see a view of Padua; a large canopy is set (R.C.) with three thrones, one a little lower than the others; the ceiling is made of long gilded beams; furniture of the period, chairs covered with gilt leather, and buffets set with gold and silver plate, and chests painted with mythological scenes. A number of the courtiers is out on the corridor looking from it down into the street below; from the street comes the roar of a mob and cries of 'Death to the Duke': after a little interval enter the Duke very calmly; he is leaning on the arm of Guido Ferranti; with him enters also the Lord Cardinal; the mob still shouting.

Duke

    No, my Lord Cardinal, I weary of her!

    Why, she is worse than ugly, she is good.

Maffio [excitedly]

    Your Grace, there are two thousand people there

    Who every moment grow more clamorous.

Duke

    Tut, man, they waste their strength upon their lungs!

    People who shout so loud, my lords, do nothing;

    The only men I fear are silent men.

                     [A yell from the people.]

    You see, Lord Cardinal, how my people love me.

                          [Another yell.]

    Go, Petrucci,

And tell the captain of the guard below

To clear the square. Do you not hear me, sir?

Do what I bid you.

[*Exit* Petrucci.]

Cardinal

I beseech your Grace

To listen to their grievances.

Duke [sitting on his throne]

Ay! the peaches

Are not so big this year as they were last.

I crave your pardon, my lord Cardinal,

I thought you spake of peaches.

[*A cheer from the people.*]

What is that?

Guido [rushes to the window]

The Duchess has gone forth into the square,

And stands between the people and the guard,

And will not let them shoot.

Duke

The devil take her!

Guido [still at the window]

And followed by a dozen of the citizens

Has come into the Palace.

Duke [starting up]

By Saint James,

Our Duchess waxes bold!

Bardi

Here comes the Duchess.

Duke

Shut that door there; this morning air is cold.

> [*They close the door on the corridor.*]

[*Enter the Duchess followed by a crowd of meanly dressed Citizens.*]

Duchess [flinging herself upon her knees]

I do beseech your Grace to give us audience.

Duke

What are these grievances?

Duchess

Alas, my Lord,

Such common things as neither you nor I,

Nor any of these noble gentlemen,

Have ever need at all to think about;

They say the bread, the very bread they eat,

Is made of sorry chaff.

First Citizen

Ay! so it is,

Nothing but chaff.

Duke

And very good food too,

I give it to my horses.

Duchess [restraining herself]

> They say the water,
>
> Set in the public cisterns for their use,
>
> [Has, through the breaking of the aqueduct,]
>
> To stagnant pools and muddy puddles turned.

Duke

> They should drink wine; water is quite unwholesome.

Second Citizen

> Alack, your Grace, the taxes which the customs
>
> Take at the city gate are grown so high
>
> We cannot buy wine.

Duke

> Then you should bless the taxes
>
> Which make you temperate.

Duchess

> Think, while we sit
>
> In gorgeous pomp and state, gaunt poverty
>
> Creeps through their sunless lanes, and with sharp knives
>
> Cuts the warm throats of children stealthily
>
> And no word said.

Third Citizen

> Ay! marry, that is true,
>
> My little son died yesternight from hunger;
>
> He was but six years old; I am so poor,
>
> I cannot bury him.

Duke

If you are poor,

Are you not blessed in that? Why, poverty

Is one of the Christian virtues,

                                [*Turns to the* Cardinal.]

Is it not?

I know, Lord Cardinal, you have great revenues,

Rich abbey-lands, and tithes, and large estates

For preaching voluntary poverty.

Duchess

Nay but, my lord the Duke, be generous;

While we sit here within a noble house

[With shaded porticoes against the sun,

And walls and roofs to keep the winter out],

There are many citizens of Padua

Who in vile tenements live so full of holes,

That the chill rain, the snow, and the rude blast,

Are tenants also with them; others sleep

Under the arches of the public bridges

All through the autumn nights, till the wet mist

Stiffens their limbs, and fevers come, and so—

Duke

And so they go to Abraham's bosom, Madam.

They should thank me for sending them to Heaven,

If they are wretched here. [To the Cardinal.]

146

Is it not said

Somewhere in Holy Writ, that every man

Should be contented with that state of life

God calls him to? Why should I change their state,

Or meddle with an all-wise providence,

Which has apportioned that some men should starve,

And others surfeit? I did not make the world.

First Citizen

He hath a hard heart.

Second Citizen

Nay, be silent, neighbour;

I think the Cardinal will speak for us.

Cardinal

True, it is Christian to bear misery,

Yet it is Christian also to be kind,

And there seem many evils in this town,

Which in your wisdom might your Grace reform.

First Citizen

What is that word reform? What does it mean?

Second Citizen

Marry, it means leaving things as they are; I like it not.

Duke

Reform Lord Cardinal, did you say reform?

There is a man in Germany called Luther,

Who would reform the Holy Catholic Church.

Have you not made him heretic, and uttered

Anathema, maranatha, against him?

Cardinal [rising from his seat]

He would have led the sheep out of the fold,

We do but ask of you to feed the sheep.

Duke

When I have shorn their fleeces I may feed them.

As for these rebels— [Duchess entreats him.]

First Citizen

That is a kind word,

He means to give us something.

Second Citizen

Is that so?

Duke

These ragged knaves who come before us here,

With mouths chock-full of treason.

Third Citizen

Good my Lord,

Fill up our mouths with bread; we'll hold our tongues.

Duke

Ye shall hold your tongues, whether you starve or not.

My lords, this age is so familiar grown,

That the low peasant hardly doffs his hat,

Unless you beat him; and the raw mechanic

Elbows the noble in the public streets.

[*To the Citizens.*]

Still as our gentle Duchess has so prayed us,

And to refuse so beautiful a beggar

Were to lack both courtesy and love,

Touching your grievances, I promise this—

First Citizen

Marry, he will lighten the taxes!

Second Citizen

Or a dole of bread, think you, for each man?

Duke

That, on next Sunday, the Lord Cardinal

Shall, after Holy Mass, preach you a sermon

Upon the Beauty of Obedience.

[*Citizens murmur.*]

First Citizen

I' faith, that will not fill our stomachs!

Second Citizen

A sermon is but a sorry sauce, when

You have nothing to eat with it.

Duchess

Poor people,

You see I have no power with the Duke,

But if you go into the court without,

My almoner shall from my private purse,

Divide a hundred ducats 'mongst you all.

First Citizen

God save the Duchess, say I.

Second Citizen

God save her.

Duchess

And every Monday morn shall bread be set

For those who lack it.

[*Citizens applaud and go out.*]

First Citizen [going out]

Why, God save the Duchess again!

Duke [calling him back]

Come hither, fellow! what is your name?

First Citizen

Dominick, sir.

Duke

A good name! Why were you called Dominick?

First Citizen [scratching his head]

Marry, because I was born on St. George's day.

Duke

A good reason! here is a ducat for you!

Will you not cry for me God save the Duke?

First Citizen [feebly]

God save the Duke.

Duke

Nay! louder, fellow, louder.

First Citizen [a little louder]

> God save the Duke!

Duke

> More lustily, fellow, put more heart in it!

> Here is another ducat for you.

First Citizen [enthusiastically]

> God save the Duke!

Duke [mockingly]

> Why, gentlemen, this simple fellow's love

> Touches me much. [To the Citizen, harshly.]

> Go! [Exit Citizen, bowing.]

> This is the way, my lords,

> You can buy popularity nowadays.

> Oh, we are nothing if not democratic!

> [To the Duchess.]

> Well, Madam,

> You spread rebellion 'midst our citizens.

Duchess

> My Lord, the poor have rights you cannot touch,

> The right to pity, and the right to mercy.

Duke

> So, so, you argue with me? This is she,

> The gentle Duchess for whose hand I yielded

> Three of the fairest towns in Italy,

> Pisa, and Genoa, and Orvieto.

Duchess

Promised, my Lord, not yielded: in that matter

Brake you your word as ever.

Duke

You wrong us, Madam,

There were state reasons.

Duchess

What state reasons are there

For breaking holy promises to a state?

Duke

There are wild boars at Pisa in a forest

Close to the city: when I promised Pisa

Unto your noble and most trusting father,

I had forgotten there was hunting there.

At Genoa they say,

Indeed I doubt them not, that the red mullet

Runs larger in the harbour of that town

Than anywhere in Italy.

[*Turning to one of the Court.*]

You, my lord,

Whose gluttonous appetite is your only god,

Could satisfy our Duchess on that point.

Duchess

And Orvieto?

Duke [yawning]

I cannot now recall

Why I did not surrender Orvieto

According to the word of my contract.

Maybe it was because I did not choose.

[*Goes over to the* Duchess.]

Why look you, Madam, you are here alone;

'Tis many a dusty league to your grey France,

And even there your father barely keeps

A hundred ragged squires for his Court.

What hope have you, I say? Which of these lords

And noble gentlemen of Padua

Stands by your side.

Duchess

There is not one.

[Guido *starts, but restrains himself.*]

Duke

Nor shall be,

While I am Duke in Padua: listen, Madam,

Being mine own, you shall do as I will,

And if it be my will you keep the house,

Why then, this palace shall your prison be;

And if it be my will you walk abroad,

Why, you shall take the air from morn to night.

Duchess

Sir, by what right—?

Duke

> Madam, my second Duchess
>
> Asked the same question once: her monument
>
> Lies in the chapel of Bartholomew,
>
> Wrought in red marble; very beautiful.
>
> Guido, your arm. Come, gentlemen, let us go
>
> And spur our falcons for the mid-day chase.
>
> Bethink you, Madam, you are here alone.
>
> > [*Exit the* Duke *leaning on* Guido, *with his Court.*]

Duchess [looking after them]

> The Duke said rightly that I was alone;
>
> Deserted, and dishonoured, and defamed,
>
> Stood ever woman so alone indeed?
>
> Men when they woo us call us pretty children,
>
> Tell us we have not wit to make our lives,
>
> And so they mar them for us. Did I say woo?
>
> We are their chattels, and their common slaves,
>
> Less dear than the poor hound that licks their hand,
>
> Less fondled than the hawk upon their wrist.
>
> Woo, did I say? bought rather, sold and bartered,
>
> Our very bodies being merchandise.
>
> I know it is the general lot of women,
>
> Each miserably mated to some man
>
> Wrecks her own life upon his selfishness:

That it is general makes it not less bitter.

I think I never heard a woman laugh,

Laugh for pure merriment, except one woman,

That was at night time, in the public streets.

Poor soul, she walked with painted lips, and wore

The mask of pleasure: I would not laugh like her;

No, death were better.

[*Enter* Guido *behind unobserved; the* Duchess *flings herself down before a picture of the Madonna.*]

O Mary mother, with your sweet pale face

Bending between the little angel heads

That hover round you, have you no help for me?

Mother of God, have you no help for me?

Guido

I can endure no longer.

This is my love, and I will speak to her.

Lady, am I a stranger to your prayers?

Duchess [rising]

None but the wretched needs my prayers, my lord.

Guido

Then must I need them, lady.

Duchess

How is that?

Does not the Duke show thee sufficient honour?

Guido

Your Grace, I lack no favours from the Duke,

Whom my soul loathes as I loathe wickedness,

But come to proffer on my bended knees,

My loyal service to thee unto death.

Duchess

Alas! I am so fallen in estate

I can but give thee a poor meed of thanks.

Guido [seizing her hand]

Hast thou no love to give me?

[*The* Duchess *starts, and* Guido *falls at her feet.*]

O dear saint,

If I have been too daring, pardon me!

Thy beauty sets my boyish blood aflame,

And, when my reverent lips touch thy white hand,

Each little nerve with such wild passion thrills

That there is nothing which I would not do

To gain thy love. [Leaps up.]

Bid me reach forth and pluck

Perilous honour from the lion's jaws,

And I will wrestle with the Nemean beast

On the bare desert! Fling to the cave of War

A gaud, a ribbon, a dead flower, something

That once has touched thee, and I'll bring it back

Though all the hosts of Christendom were there,

Inviolate again! ay, more than this,

Set me to scale the pallid white-faced cliffs

Of mighty England, and from that arrogant shield

Will I raze out the lilies of your France

Which England, that sea-lion of the sea,

Hath taken from her!

O dear Beatrice,

Drive me not from thy presence! without thee

The heavy minutes crawl with feet of lead,

But, while I look upon thy loveliness,

The hours fly like winged Mercuries

And leave existence golden.

Duchess

I did not think

I should be ever loved: do you indeed

Love me so much as now you say you do?

Guido

Ask of the sea-bird if it loves the sea,

Ask of the roses if they love the rain,

Ask of the little lark, that will not sing

Till day break, if it loves to see the day:—

And yet, these are but empty images,

Mere shadows of my love, which is a fire

So great that all the waters of the main

Can not avail to quench it. Will you not speak?

Duchess

I hardly know what I should say to you.

Guido

Will you not say you love me?

Duchess

Is that my lesson?

Must I say all at once? 'Twere a good lesson

If I did love you, sir; but, if I do not,

What shall I say then?

Guido

If you do not love me,

Say, none the less, you do, for on your tongue

Falsehood for very shame would turn to truth.

Duchess

What if I do not speak at all? They say

Lovers are happiest when they are in doubt

Guido

Nay, doubt would kill me, and if I must die,

Why, let me die for joy and not for doubt.

Oh, tell me may I stay, or must I go?

Duchess

I would not have you either stay or go;

For if you stay you steal my love from me,

And if you go you take my love away.

Guido, though all the morning stars could sing

They could not tell the measure of my love.

I love you, Guido.

Guido [stretching out his hands]

Oh, do not cease at all;

I thought the nightingale sang but at night;

Or if thou needst must cease, then let my lips

Touch the sweet lips that can such music make.

Duchess

To touch my lips is not to touch my heart.

Guido

Do you close that against me?

Duchess

Alas! my lord,

I have it not: the first day that I saw you

I let you take my heart away from me;

Unwilling thief, that without meaning it

Did break into my fenced treasury

And filch my jewel from it! O strange theft,

Which made you richer though you knew it not,

And left me poorer, and yet glad of it!

Guido [clasping her in his arms]

O love, love, love! Nay, sweet, lift up your head,

Let me unlock those little scarlet doors

That shut in music, let me dive for coral

In your red lips, and I'll bear back a prize

Richer than all the gold the Gryphon guards

In rude Armenia.

Duchess

You are my lord,

And what I have is yours, and what I have not

Your fancy lends me, like a prodigal

Spending its wealth on what is nothing worth.

[*Kisses him.*]

Guido

Methinks I am bold to look upon you thus:

The gentle violet hides beneath its leaf

And is afraid to look at the great sun

For fear of too much splendour, but my eyes,

O daring eyes! are grown so venturous

That like fixed stars they stand, gazing at you,

And surfeit sense with beauty.

Duchess

Dear love, I would

You could look upon me ever, for your eyes

Are polished mirrors, and when I peer

Into those mirrors I can see myself,

And so I know my image lives in you.

Guido [taking her in his arms]

Stand still, thou hurrying orb in the high heavens,

And make this hour immortal! [A pause.]

Duchess

Sit down here,

A little lower than me: yes, just so, sweet,

That I may run my fingers through your hair,

And see your face turn upwards like a flower

To meet my kiss.

Have you not sometimes noted,

When we unlock some long-disuséd room

With heavy dust and soiling mildew filled,

Where never foot of man has come for years,

And from the windows take the rusty bar,

And fling the broken shutters to the air,

And let the bright sun in, how the good sun

Turns every grimy particle of dust

Into a little thing of dancing gold?

Guido, my heart is that long-empty room,

But you have let love in, and with its gold

Gilded all life. Do you not think that love

Fills up the sum of life?

Guido

Ay! without love

Life is no better than the unhewn stone

Which in the quarry lies, before the sculptor

Has set the God within it. Without love

Life is as silent as the common reeds

That through the marshes or by rivers grow,

And have no music in them.

Duchess

Yet out of these

The singer, who is Love, will make a pipe

And from them he draws music; so I think

Love will bring music out of any life.

Is that not true?

Guido

Sweet, women make it true.

There are men who paint pictures, and carve statues,

Paul of Verona and the dyer's son,

Or their great rival, who, by the sea at Venice,

Has set God's little maid upon the stair,

White as her own white lily, and as tall,

Or Raphael, whose Madonnas are divine

Because they are mothers merely; yet I think

Women are the best artists of the world,

For they can take the common lives of men

Soiled with the money-getting of our age,

And with love make them beautiful.

Duchess

Ah, dear,

I wish that you and I were very poor;

The poor, who love each other, are so rich.

Guido

Tell me again you love me, Beatrice.

Duchess [fingering his collar]

How well this collar lies about your throat.

[Lord Moranzone *looks through the door from the corridor outside.*]

Guido

Nay, tell me that you love me.

Duchess

I remember,

That when I was a child in my dear France,

Being at Court at Fontainebleau, the King

Wore such a collar.

Guido

Will you not say you love me?

Duchess [smiling]

He was a very royal man, King Francis,

Yet he was not royal as you are.

Why need I tell you, Guido, that I love you?

[*Takes his head in her hands and turns his face up to her.*]

Do you not know that I am yours for ever,

Body and soul?

[*Kisses him, and then suddenly catches sight of Moranzone and leaps up.*]

    Oh, what is that? [Moranzone disappears.]

Guido

    What, love?

Duchess

    Methought I saw a face with eyes of flame

    Look at us through the doorway.

Guido

    Nay, 'twas nothing:

    The passing shadow of the man on guard.

        [*The* Duchess *still stands looking at the window.*]

    'Twas nothing, sweet.

Duchess

    Ay! what can harm us now,

    Who are in Love's hand? I do not think I'd care

    Though the vile world should with its lackey Slander

    Trample and tread upon my life; why should I?

    They say the common field-flowers of the field

    Have sweeter scent when they are trodden on

    Than when they bloom alone, and that some herbs

    Which have no perfume, on being bruiséd die

    With all Arabia round them; so it is

    With the young lives this dull world seeks to crush,

    It does but bring the sweetness out of them,

    And makes them lovelier often. And besides,

While we have love we have the best of life:

Is it not so?

Guido

Dear, shall we play or sing?

I think that I could sing now.

Duchess

Do not speak,

For there are times when all existences

Seem narrowed to one single ecstasy,

And Passion sets a seal upon the lips.

Guido

Oh, with mine own lips let me break that seal!

You love me, Beatrice?

Duchess

Ay! is it not strange

I should so love mine enemy?

Guido

Who is he?

Duchess

Why, you: that with your shaft did pierce my heart!

Poor heart, that lived its little lonely life

Until it met your arrow.

Guido

Ah, dear love,

I am so wounded by that bolt myself

That with untended wounds I lie a-dying,

Unless you cure me, dear Physician.

Duchess

I would not have you cured; for I am sick

With the same malady.

Guido

Oh, how I love you!

See, I must steal the cuckoo's voice, and tell

The one tale over.

Duchess

Tell no other tale!

For, if that is the little cuckoo's song,

The nightingale is hoarse, and the loud lark

Has lost its music.

Guido

Kiss me, Beatrice!

[*She takes his face in her hands and bends down and kisses him; a loud knocking then comes at the door, and* Guido *leaps up; enter a Servant.*]

Servant

A package for you, sir.

Guido [carelessly]

Ah! give it to me.

[*Servant hands package wrapped in vermilion silk, and exit; as Guido is about to open it the Duchess comes up behind, and in sport takes it from him.*]

Duchess [laughing]

Now I will wager it is from some girl

Who would have you wear her favour; I am so jealous

I will not give up the least part in you,

But like a miser keep you to myself,

And spoil you perhaps in keeping.

Guido

It is nothing.

Duchess

Nay, it is from some girl.

Guido

You know 'tis not.

Duchess [turns her back and opens it]

Now, traitor, tell me what does this sign mean,

A dagger with two leopards wrought in steel?

Guido [taking it from her]

O God!

Duchess

I'll from the window look, and try

If I can't see the porter's livery

Who left it at the gate! I will not rest

Till I have learned your secret.

> [*Runs laughing into the corridor.*]

Guido

Oh, horrible!

Had I so soon forgot my father's death,

Did I so soon let love into my heart,

167

And must I banish love, and let in murder

That beats and clamours at the outer gate?

Ay, that I must! Have I not sworn an oath?

Yet not to-night; nay, it must be to-night.

Farewell then all the joy and light of life,

All dear recorded memories, farewell,

Farewell all love! Could I with bloody hands

Fondle and paddle with her innocent hands?

Could I with lips fresh from this butchery

Play with her lips? Could I with murderous eyes

Look in those violet eyes, whose purity

Would strike men blind, and make each eyeball reel

In night perpetual? No, murder has set

A barrier between us far too high

For us to kiss across it.

Duchess

Guido!

Guido

Beatrice,

You must forget that name, and banish me

Out of your life for ever.

Duchess [going towards him]

O dear love!

Guido [stepping back]

There lies a barrier between us two

We dare not pass.

Duchess

I dare do anything

So that you are beside me.

Guido

Ah! There it is,

I cannot be beside you, cannot breathe

The air you breathe; I cannot any more

Stand face to face with beauty, which unnerves

My shaking heart, and makes my desperate hand

Fail of its purpose. Let me go hence, I pray;

Forget you ever looked upon me.

Duchess

What!

With your hot kisses fresh upon my lips

Forget the vows of love you made to me?

Guido

I take them back.

Duchess

Alas, you cannot, Guido,

For they are part of nature now; the air

Is tremulous with their music, and outside

The little birds sing sweeter for those vows.

Guido

There lies a barrier between us now,

Which then I knew not, or I had forgot.

Duchess

There is no barrier, Guido; why, I will go

In poor attire, and will follow you

Over the world.

Guido [wildly]

The world's not wide enough

To hold us two! Farewell, farewell for ever.

Duchess [calm, and controlling her passion]

Why did you come into my life at all, then,

Or in the desolate garden of my heart

Sow that white flower of love—?

Guido

O Beatrice!

Duchess

Which now you would dig up, uproot, tear out,

Though each small fibre doth so hold my heart

That if you break one, my heart breaks with it?

Why did you come into my life? Why open

The secret wells of love I had sealed up?

Why did you open them—?

Guido

O God!

Duchess [clenching her hand]

And let

The floodgates of my passion swell and burst

Till, like the wave when rivers overflow

That sweeps the forest and the farm away,

Love in the splendid avalanche of its might

Swept my life with it? Must I drop by drop

Gather these waters back and seal them up?

Alas! Each drop will be a tear, and so

Will with its saltness make life very bitter.

Guido

I pray you speak no more, for I must go

Forth from your life and love, and make a way

On which you cannot follow.

Duchess

I have heard

That sailors dying of thirst upon a raft,

Poor castaways upon a lonely sea,

Dream of green fields and pleasant water-courses,

And then wake up with red thirst in their throats,

And die more miserably because sleep

Has cheated them: so they die cursing sleep

For having sent them dreams: I will not curse you

Though I am cast away upon the sea

Which men call Desolation.

Guido

>O God, God!

Duchess

>But you will stay: listen, I love you, Guido.

>[*She waits a little.*]

>Is echo dead, that when I say I love you

>There is no answer?

Guido

>Everything is dead,

>Save one thing only, which shall die to-night!

Duchess

>If you are going, touch me not, but go.

>[*Exit* Guido.]

Barrier! Barrier!

>Why did he say there was a barrier?

>There is no barrier between us two.

>He lied to me, and shall I for that reason

>Loathe what I love, and what I worshipped, hate?

>I think we women do not love like that.

>For if I cut his image from my heart,

>My heart would, like a bleeding pilgrim, follow

>That image through the world, and call it back

>With little cries of love.

[*Enter* Duke *equipped for the chase, with falconers and hounds.*]

Duke

Madam, you keep us waiting;

You keep my dogs waiting.

Duchess

I will not ride to-day.

Duke

How now, what's this?

Duchess

My Lord, I cannot go.

Duke

What, pale face, do you dare to stand against me?

Why, I could set you on a sorry jade

And lead you through the town, till the low rabble

You feed toss up their hats and mock at you.

Duchess

Have you no word of kindness ever for me?

Duke

I hold you in the hollow of my hand

And have no need on you to waste kind words.

Duchess

Well, I will go.

Duke [slapping his boot with his whip]

No, I have changed my mind,

You will stay here, and like a faithful wife

Watch from the window for our coming back.

Were it not dreadful if some accident

By chance should happen to your loving Lord?

Come, gentlemen, my hounds begin to chafe,

And I chafe too, having a patient wife.

Where is young Guido?

Maffio

My liege, I have not seen him

For a full hour past.

Duke

It matters not,

I dare say I shall see him soon enough.

Well, Madam, you will sit at home and spin.

I do protest, sirs, the domestic virtues

Are often very beautiful in others.

[Exit Duke with his Court.]

Duchess

The stars have fought against me, that is all,

And thus to-night when my Lord lieth asleep,

Will I fall upon my dagger, and so cease.

My heart is such a stone nothing can reach it

Except the dagger's edge: let it go there,

To find what name it carries: ay! to-night

Death will divorce the Duke; and yet to-night

He may die also, he is very old.

Why should he not die? Yesterday his hand

Shook with a palsy: men have died from palsy,

And why not he? Are there not fevers also,

Agues and chills, and other maladies

Most incident to old age?

No, no, he will not die, he is too sinful;

Honest men die before their proper time.

Good men will die: men by whose side the Duke

In all the sick pollution of his life

Seems like a leper: women and children die,

But the Duke will not die, he is too sinful.

Oh, can it be

There is some immortality in sin,

Which virtue has not? And does the wicked man

Draw life from what to other men were death,

Like poisonous plants that on corruption live?

No, no, I think God would not suffer that:

Yet the Duke will not die: he is too sinful.

But I will die alone, and on this night

Grim Death shall be my bridegroom, and the tomb

My secret house of pleasure: well, what of that?

The world's a graveyard, and we each, like coffins,

Within us bear a skeleton.

[*Enter* Lord Moranzone *all in black; he passes across the back of the stage*

175

looking anxiously about.]

Moranzone

Where is Guido?

I cannot find him anywhere.

Duchess [catches sight of him]

O God!

'Twas thou who took my love away from me.

Moranzone [with a look of joy]

What, has he left you?

Duchess

Nay, you know he has.

Oh, give him back to me, give him back, I say,

Or I will tear your body limb from limb,

And to the common gibbet nail your head

Until the carrion crows have stripped it bare.

Better you had crossed a hungry lioness

Before you came between me and my love.

[*With more pathos.*]

Nay, give him back, you know not how I love him.

Here by this chair he knelt a half hour since;

'Twas there he stood, and there he looked at me;

This is the hand he kissed, and these the ears

Into whose open portals he did pour

A tale of love so musical that all

The birds stopped singing! Oh, give him back to me.

Moranzone

He does not love you, Madam.

Duchess

May the plague

Wither the tongue that says so! Give him back.

Moranzone

Madam, I tell you you will never see him,

Neither to-night, nor any other night.

Duchess

What is your name?

Moranzone

My name? Revenge!

[*Exit.*]

Duchess

Revenge!

I think I never harmed a little child.

What should Revenge do coming to my door?

It matters not, for Death is there already,

Waiting with his dim torch to light my way.

'Tis true men hate thee, Death, and yet I think

Thou wilt be kinder to me than my lover,

And so dispatch the messengers at once,

Harry the lazy steeds of lingering day,

And let the night, thy sister, come instead,

And drape the world in mourning; let the owl,

Who is thy minister, scream from his tower

And wake the toad with hooting, and the bat,

That is the slave of dim Persephone,

Wheel through the sombre air on wandering wing!

Tear up the shrieking mandrakes from the earth

And bid them make us music, and tell the mole

To dig deep down thy cold and narrow bed,

For I shall lie within thine arms to-night.

END OF ACT II.

ACT III

SCENE

A large corridor in the Ducal Palace: a window (L.C.) looks out on a view of Padua by moonlight: a staircase (R.C.) leads up to a door with a portière of crimson velvet, with the Duke's arms embroidered in gold on it: on the lowest step of the staircase a figure draped in black is sitting: the hall is lit by an iron cresset filled with burning tow: thunder and lightning outside: the time is night.

[*Enter* Guido *through the window.*]

Guido

The wind is rising: how my ladder shook!

I thought that every gust would break the cords!

[Looks out at the city.]

Christ! What a night:

Great thunder in the heavens, and wild lightnings

Striking from pinnacle to pinnacle

Across the city, till the dim houses seem

To shudder and to shake as each new glare

Dashes adown the street.

[Passes across the stage to foot of staircase.]

Ah! who art thou

That sittest on the stair, like unto Death

Waiting a guilty soul? [A pause.]

Canst thou not speak?

Or has this storm laid palsy on thy tongue,

And chilled thy utterance?

[The figure rises and takes off his mask.]

Moranzone

Guido Ferranti,

Thy murdered father laughs for joy to-night.

Guido [confusedly]

What, art thou here?

Moranzone

Ay, waiting for your coming.

Guido [looking away from him]

I did not think to see you, but am glad,

That you may know the thing I mean to do.

Moranzone

First, I would have you know my well-laid plans;

Listen: I have set horses at the gate

Which leads to Parma: when you have done your business

We will ride hence, and by to-morrow night—

Guido

It cannot be.

Moranzone

Nay, but it shall.

Guido

Listen, Lord Moranzone,

I am resolved not to kill this man.

Moranzone

Surely my ears are traitors, speak again:

It cannot be but age has dulled my powers,

I am an old man now: what did you say?

You said that with that dagger in your belt

You would avenge your father's bloody murder;

Did you not say that?

Guido

No, my lord, I said

I was resolved not to kill the Duke.

Moranzone

You said not that; it is my senses mock me;

Or else this midnight air o'ercharged with storm

Alters your message in the giving it.

Guido

Nay, you heard rightly; I'll not kill this man.

Moranzone

What of thine oath, thou traitor, what of thine oath?

Guido

I am resolved not to keep that oath.

Moranzone

What of thy murdered father?

Guido

Dost thou think

My father would be glad to see me coming,

This old man's blood still hot upon mine hands?

Moranzone

Ay! he would laugh for joy.

Guido

I do not think so,

There is better knowledge in the other world;

Vengeance is God's, let God himself revenge.

Moranzone

Thou art God's minister of vengeance.

Guido

No!

God hath no minister but his own hand.

I will not kill this man.

Moranzone

Why are you here,

If not to kill him, then?

Guido

Lord Moranzone,

I purpose to ascend to the Duke's chamber,

And as he lies asleep lay on his breast

The dagger and this writing; when he awakes

Then he will know who held him in his power

And slew him not: this is the noblest vengeance

Which I can take.

Moranzone

You will not slay him?

Guido

No.

Moranzone

Ignoble son of a noble father,

Who sufferest this man who sold that father

To live an hour.

Guido

'Twas thou that hindered me;

I would have killed him in the open square,

The day I saw him first.

Moranzone

It was not yet time;

Now it is time, and, like some green-faced girl,

Thou pratest of forgiveness.

Guido

No! revenge:

The right revenge my father's son should take.

Moranzone

You are a coward,

Take out the knife, get to the Duke's chamber,

And bring me back his heart upon the blade.

When he is dead, then you can talk to me

Of noble vengeances.

Guido

Upon thine honour,

And by the love thou bearest my father's name,

Dost thou think my father, that great gentleman,

That generous soldier, that most chivalrous lord,

Would have crept at night-time, like a common thief,

And stabbed an old man sleeping in his bed,

However he had wronged him: tell me that.

Moranzone

[after some hesitation]

You have sworn an oath, see that you keep that oath.

Boy, do you think I do not know your secret,

Your traffic with the Duchess?

Guido

Silence, liar!

The very moon in heaven is not more chaste.

Nor the white stars so pure.

Moranzone

And yet, you love her;

Weak fool, to let love in upon your life,

Save as a plaything.

Guido

You do well to talk:

Within your veins, old man, the pulse of youth

Throbs with no ardour. Your eyes full of rheum

Have against Beauty closed their filmy doors,

And your clogged ears, losing their natural sense,

184

Have shut you from the music of the world.

You talk of love! You know not what it is.

Moranzone

Oh, in my time, boy, have I walked i' the moon,

Swore I would live on kisses and on blisses,

Swore I would die for love, and did not die,

Wrote love bad verses; ay, and sung them badly,

Like all true lovers: Oh, I have done the tricks!

I know the partings and the chamberings;

We are all animals at best, and love

Is merely passion with a holy name.

Guido

Now then I know you have not loved at all.

Love is the sacrament of life; it sets

Virtue where virtue was not; cleanses men

Of all the vile pollutions of this world;

It is the fire which purges gold from dross,

It is the fan which winnows wheat from chaff,

It is the spring which in some wintry soil

Makes innocence to blossom like a rose.

The days are over when God walked with men,

But Love, which is his image, holds his place.

When a man loves a woman, then he knows

God's secret, and the secret of the world.

There is no house so lowly or so mean,

Which, if their hearts be pure who live in it,

Love will not enter; but if bloody murder

Knock at the Palace gate and is let in,

Love like a wounded thing creeps out and dies.

This is the punishment God sets on sin.

The wicked cannot love.

    [*A groan comes from the* Duke's *chamber.*]

Ah! What is that?

Do you not hear? 'Twas nothing.

So I think

That it is woman's mission by their love

To save the souls of men: and loving her,

My Lady, my white Beatrice, I begin

To see a nobler and a holier vengeance

In letting this man live, than doth reside

In bloody deeds o' night, stabs in the dark,

And young hands clutching at a palsied throat.

It was, I think, for love's sake that Lord Christ,

Who was indeed himself incarnate Love,

Bade every man forgive his enemy.

Moranzone [sneeringly]

That was in Palestine, not Padua;

And said for saints: I have to do with men.

Guido

It was for all time said.

Moranzone

And your white Duchess,

What will she do to thank you?

Guido

Alas, I will not see her face again.

'Tis but twelve hours since I parted from her,

So suddenly, and with such violent passion,

That she has shut her heart against me now:

No, I will never see her.

Moranzone

What will you do?

Guido

After that I have laid the dagger there,

Get hence to-night from Padua.

Moranzone

And then?

Guido

I will take service with the Doge at Venice,

And bid him pack me straightway to the wars,

And there I will, being now sick of life,

Throw that poor life against some desperate spear.

[*A groan from the* Duke's *chamber again.*]

Did you not hear a voice?

Moranzone

> I always hear,
>
> From the dim confines of some sepulchre,
>
> A voice that cries for vengeance. We waste time,
>
> It will be morning soon; are you resolved
>
> You will not kill the Duke?

Guido

> I am resolved.

Moranzone

> O wretched father, lying unavenged.

Guido

> More wretched, were thy son a murderer.

Moranzone

> Why, what is life?

Guido

> I do not know, my lord,
>
> I did not give it, and I dare not take it.

Moranzone

> I do not thank God often; but I think
>
> I thank him now that I have got no son!
>
> And you, what bastard blood flows in your veins
>
> That when you have your enemy in your grasp
>
> You let him go! I would that I had left you
>
> With the dull hinds that reared you.

Guido

Better perhaps

That you had done so! May be better still

I'd not been born to this distressful world.

Moranzone

Farewell!

Guido

Farewell! Some day, Lord Moranzone,

You will understand my vengeance.

Moranzone

Never, boy.

[*Gets out of window and exit by rope ladder.*]

Guido

Father, I think thou knowest my resolve,

And with this nobler vengeance art content.

Father, I think in letting this man live

That I am doing what thou wouldst have done.

Father, I know not if a human voice

Can pierce the iron gateway of the dead,

Or if the dead are set in ignorance

Of what we do, or do not, for their sakes.

And yet I feel a presence in the air,

There is a shadow standing at my side,

And ghostly kisses seem to touch my lips,

And leave them holier. [Kneels down.]

O father, if 'tis thou,

Canst thou not burst through the decrees of death,

And if corporeal semblance show thyself,

That I may touch thy hand!

No, there is nothing. [Rises.]

'Tis the night that cheats us with its phantoms,

And, like a puppet-master, makes us think

That things are real which are not. It grows late.

Now must I to my business.

> [*Pulls out a letter from his doublet and reads it.*]

When he wakes,

And sees this letter, and the dagger with it,

Will he not have some loathing for his life,

Repent, perchance, and lead a better life,

Or will he mock because a young man spared

His natural enemy? I do not care.

Father, it is thy bidding that I do,

Thy bidding, and the bidding of my love

Which teaches me to know thee as thou art.

[*Ascends staircase stealthily, and just as he reaches out his hand to draw back the curtain the Duchess appears all in white. Guido starts back.*]

Duchess

Guido! what do you here so late?

Guido

O white and spotless angel of my life,

Sure thou hast come from Heaven with a message

That mercy is more noble than revenge?

Duchess

There is no barrier between us now.

Guido

None, love, nor shall be.

Duchess

I have seen to that.

Guido

Tarry here for me.

Duchess

No, you are not going?

You will not leave me as you did before?

Guido

I will return within a moment's space,

But first I must repair to the Duke's chamber,

And leave this letter and this dagger there,

That when he wakes—

Duchess

When who wakes?

Guido

Why, the Duke.

Duchess

He will not wake again.

Guido

What, is he dead?

Duchess

Ay! he is dead.

Guido

O God! how wonderful

Are all thy secret ways! Who would have said

That on this very night, when I had yielded

Into thy hands the vengeance that is thine,

Thou with thy finger wouldst have touched the man,

And bade him come before thy judgment seat.

Duchess

I have just killed him.

Guido [in horror]

Oh!

Duchess

He was asleep;

Come closer, love, and I will tell you all.

I had resolved to kill myself to-night.

About an hour ago I waked from sleep,

And took my dagger from beneath my pillow,

Where I had hidden it to serve my need,

And drew it from the sheath, and felt the edge,

And thought of you, and how I loved you, Guido,

And turned to fall upon it, when I marked

The old man sleeping, full of years and sin;

There lay he muttering curses in his sleep,

And as I looked upon his evil face

Suddenly like a flame there flashed across me,

There is the barrier which Guido spoke of:

You said there lay a barrier between us,

What barrier but he?—

I hardly know

What happened, but a steaming mist of blood

Rose up between us two.

Guido

Oh, horrible!

Duchess

And then he groaned,

And then he groaned no more! I only heard

The dripping of the blood upon the floor.

Guido

Enough, enough.

Duchess

Will you not kiss me now?

Do you remember saying that women's love

Turns men to angels? well, the love of man

Turns women into martyrs; for its sake

We do or suffer anything.

Guido

O God!

Duchess

 Will you not speak?

Guido

 I cannot speak at all.

Duchess

 Let as not talk of this! Let us go hence:

 Is not the barrier broken down between us?

 What would you more? Come, it is almost morning.

          [*Puts her hand on* Guido's.]

Guido [breaking from her]

 O damned saint! O angel fresh from Hell!

 What bloody devil tempted thee to this!

 That thou hast killed thy husband, that is nothing—

 Hell was already gaping for his soul—

 But thou hast murdered Love, and in its place

 Hast set a horrible and bloodstained thing,

 Whose very breath breeds pestilence and plague,

 And strangles Love.

Duchess [in amazed wonder]

 I did it all for you.

 I would not have you do it, had you willed it,

 For I would keep you without blot or stain,

 A thing unblemished, unassailed, untarnished.

 Men do not know what women do for love.

 Have I not wrecked my soul for your dear sake,

Here and hereafter?

Guido

No, do not touch me,

Between us lies a thin red stream of blood;

I dare not look across it: when you stabbed him

You stabbed Love with a sharp knife to the heart.

We cannot meet again.

Duchess [wringing her hands]

For you! For you!

I did it all for you: have you forgotten?

You said there was a barrier between us;

That barrier lies now i' the upper chamber

Upset, overthrown, beaten, and battered down,

And will not part us ever.

Guido

No, you mistook:

Sin was the barrier, you have raised it up;

Crime was the barrier, you have set it there.

The barrier was murder, and your hand

Has builded it so high it shuts out heaven,

It shuts out God.

Duchess

I did it all for you;

You dare not leave me now: nay, Guido, listen.

Get horses ready, we will fly to-night.

The past is a bad dream, we will forget it:

Before us lies the future: shall we not have

Sweet days of love beneath our vines and laugh?—

No, no, we will not laugh, but, when we weep,

Well, we will weep together; I will serve you;

I will be very meek and very gentle:

You do not know me.

Guido

Nay, I know you now;

Get hence, I say, out of my sight.

Duchess [pacing up and down]

O God,

How I have loved this man!

Guido

You never loved me.

Had it been so, Love would have stayed your hand.

How could we sit together at Love's table?

You have poured poison in the sacred wine,

And Murder dips his fingers in the sop.

Duchess [throws herself on her knees]

Then slay me now! I have spilt blood to-night,

You shall spill more, so we go hand in hand

To heaven or to hell. Draw your sword, Guido.

Quick, let your soul go chambering in my heart,

It will but find its master's image there.

Nay, if you will not slay me with your sword,

Bid me to fall upon this reeking knife,

And I will do it.

Guido [wresting knife from her]

Give it to me, I say.

O God, your very hands are wet with blood!

This place is Hell, I cannot tarry here.

I pray you let me see your face no more.

Duchess

Better for me I had not seen your face.

[Guido *recoils: she seizes his hands as she kneels.*]

Nay, Guido, listen for a while:

Until you came to Padua I lived

Wretched indeed, but with no murderous thought,

Very submissive to a cruel Lord,

Very obedient to unjust commands,

As pure I think as any gentle girl

Who now would turn in horror from my hands—

[*Stands up.*]

You came: ah! Guido, the first kindly words

I ever heard since I had come from France

Were from your lips: well, well, that is no matter.

You came, and in the passion of your eyes

I read love's meaning; everything you said

Touched my dumb soul to music, so I loved you.

And yet I did not tell you of my love.

'Twas you who sought me out, knelt at my feet

As I kneel now at yours, and with sweet vows,

[Kneels.]

Whose music seems to linger in my ears,

Swore that you loved me, and I trusted you.

I think there are many women in the world

Who would have tempted you to kill the man.

I did not.

Yet I know that had I done so,

I had not been thus humbled in the dust,

[Stands up.]

But you had loved me very faithfully.

[After a pause approaches him timidly.]

I do not think you understand me, Guido:

It was for your sake that I wrought this deed

Whose horror now chills my young blood to ice,

For your sake only. [Stretching out her arm.]

Will you not speak to me?

Love me a little: in my girlish life

I have been starved for love, and kindliness

Has passed me by.

Guido

> I dare not look at you:
>
> You come to me with too pronounced a favour;
>
> Get to your tirewomen.

Duchess

> Ay, there it is!
>
> There speaks the man! yet had you come to me
>
> With any heavy sin upon your soul,
>
> Some murder done for hire, not for love,
>
> Why, I had sat and watched at your bedside
>
> All through the night-time, lest Remorse might come
>
> And pour his poisons in your ear, and so
>
> Keep you from sleeping! Sure it is the guilty,
>
> Who, being very wretched, need love most.

Guido

> There is no love where there is any guilt.

Duchess

> No love where there is any guilt! O God,
>
> How differently do we love from men!
>
> There is many a woman here in Padua,
>
> Some workman's wife, or ruder artisan's,
>
> Whose husband spends the wages of the week
>
> In a coarse revel, or a tavern brawl,

And reeling home late on the Saturday night,

Finds his wife sitting by a fireless hearth,

Trying to hush the child who cries for hunger,

And then sets to and beats his wife because

The child is hungry, and the fire black.

Yet the wife loves him! and will rise next day

With some red bruise across a careworn face,

And sweep the house, and do the common service,

And try and smile, and only be too glad

If he does not beat her a second time

Before her child!—that is how women love.

                          [*A pause:* Guido *says nothing.*]

I think you will not drive me from your side.

Where have I got to go if you reject me?—

You for whose sake this hand has murdered life,

You for whose sake my soul has wrecked itself

Beyond all hope of pardon.

Guido

Get thee gone:

The dead man is a ghost, and our love too,

Flits like a ghost about its desolate tomb,

And wanders through this charnel house, and weeps

That when you slew your lord you slew it also.

Do you not see?

Duchess

    I see when men love women

    They give them but a little of their lives,

    But women when they love give everything;

    I see that, Guido, now.

Guido

    Away, away,

    And come not back till you have waked your dead.

Duchess

    I would to God that I could wake the dead,

    Put vision in the glazéd eves, and give

    The tongue its natural utterance, and bid

    The heart to beat again: that cannot be:

    For what is done, is done: and what is dead

    Is dead for ever: the fire cannot warm him:

    The winter cannot hurt him with its snows;

    Something has gone from him; if you call him now,

    He will not answer; if you mock him now,

    He will not laugh; and if you stab him now

    He will not bleed.

    I would that I could wake him!

    O God, put back the sun a little space,

    And from the roll of time blot out to-night,

    And bid it not have been! Put back the sun,

And make me what I was an hour ago!

No, no, time will not stop for anything,

Nor the sun stay its courses, though Repentance

Calling it back grow hoarse; but you, my love,

Have you no word of pity even for me?

O Guido, Guido, will you not kiss me once?

Drive me not to some desperate resolve:

Women grow mad when they are treated thus:

Will you not kiss me once?

Guido [holding up knife]

I will not kiss you

Until the blood grows dry upon this knife,

[Wildly] Back to your dead!

Duchess [going up the stairs]

Why, then I will be gone! and may you find

More mercy than you showed to me to-night!

Guido

Let me find mercy when I go at night

And do foul murder.

Duchess [coming down a few steps.]

Murder did you say?

Murder is hungry, and still cries for more,

And Death, his brother, is not satisfied,

But walks the house, and will not go away,

Unless he has a comrade! Tarry, Death,

For I will give thee a most faithful lackey

To travel with thee! Murder, call no more,

For thou shalt eat thy fill.

There is a storm

Will break upon this house before the morning,

So horrible, that the white moon already

Turns grey and sick with terror, the low wind

Goes moaning round the house, and the high stars

Run madly through the vaulted firmament,

As though the night wept tears of liquid fire

For what the day shall look upon. Oh, weep,

Thou lamentable heaven! Weep thy fill!

Though sorrow like a cataract drench the fields,

And make the earth one bitter lake of tears,

It would not be enough. [A peal of thunder.]

Do you not hear,

There is artillery in the Heaven to-night.

Vengeance is wakened up, and has unloosed

His dogs upon the world, and in this matter

Which lies between us two, let him who draws

The thunder on his head beware the ruin

Which the forked flame brings after.

[*A flash of lightning followed by a peal of thunder.*]

Guido

    Away! away!

[Exit the Duchess, who as she lifts the crimson curtain looks back for a moment at Guido, but he makes no sign. More thunder.]

    Now is life fallen in ashes at my feet

    And noble love self-slain; and in its place

    Crept murder with its silent bloody feet.

    And she who wrought it—Oh! and yet she loved me,

    And for my sake did do this dreadful thing.

    I have been cruel to her: Beatrice!

    Beatrice, I say, come back.

[*Begins to ascend staircase, when the noise of Soldiers is heard.*]

    Ah! what is that?

    Torches ablaze, and noise of hurrying feet.

    Pray God they have not seized her.

                      [*Noise grows louder.*]

    Beatrice!

    There is yet time to escape. Come down, come out!

          [*The voice of the* Duchess *outside.*]

    This way went he, the man who slew my lord.

[*Down the staircase comes hurrying a confused body of Soldiers;* Guido *is not seen at first, till the* Duchess *surrounded by Servants carrying torches appears at the top of the staircase, and points to Guido, who is seized at once, one of the Soldiers dragging the knife from his hand and showing it to the Captain of the Guard in sight of the audience. Tableau.*]

END OF ACT III.

ACT IV

SCENE

The Court of Justice: the walls are hung with stamped grey velvet: above the hangings the wall is red, and gilt symbolical figures bear up the roof, which is made of red beams with grey soffits and moulding: a canopy of white satin flowered with gold is set for the Duchess: below it a long bench with red cloth for the Judges: below that a table for the clerks of the court. Two soldiers stand on each side of the canopy, and two soldiers guard the door; the citizens have some of them collected in the Court; others are coming in greeting one another; two tipstaffs in violet keep order with long white wands.

First Citizen

Good morrow, neighbour Anthony.

Second Citizen

Good morrow, neighbour Dominick.

First Citizen

This is a strange day for Padua, is it not?—the Duke being dead.

Second Citizen

I tell you, neighbour Dominick, I have not known such a day since the last Duke died.

First Citizen

They will try him first, and sentence him afterwards, will they not, neighbour Anthony?

Second Citizen

Nay, for he might 'scape his punishment then; but they will condemn him first so that he gets his deserts, and give him trial afterwards so that no injustice is done.

First Citizen

Well, well, it will go hard with him I doubt not.

Second Citizen

Surely it is a grievous thing to shed a Duke's blood.

Third Citizen

They say a Duke has blue blood.

Second Citizen

I think our Duke's blood was black like his soul.

First Citizen

Have a watch, neighbour Anthony, the officer is looking at thee.

Second Citizen

I care not if he does but look at me; he cannot whip me with the lashes of his eye.

Third Citizen

What think you of this young man who stuck the knife into the Duke?

Second Citizen

Why, that he is a well-behaved, and a well-meaning, and a well-favoured lad, and yet wicked in that he killed the Duke.

Third Citizen

'Twas the first time he did it: may be the law will not be hard on him, as he did not do it before.

Second Citizen

True.

Tipstaff

Silence, knave.

Second Citizen

Am I thy looking-glass, Master Tipstaff, that thou callest me knave?

First Citizen

Here be one of the household coming. Well, Dame Lucy, thou art of the Court, how does thy poor mistress the Duchess, with her sweet face?

Mistress Lucy

O well-a-day! O miserable day! O day! O misery! Why it is just nineteen years last June, at Michaelmas, since I was married to my husband, and it is August now, and here is the Duke murdered; there is a coincidence for you!

Second Citizen

Why, if it is a coincidence, they may not kill the young man: there is no law against coincidences.

First Citizen

But how does the Duchess?

Mistress Lucy

Well well, I knew some harm would happen to the house: six weeks ago the cakes were all burned on one side, and last Saint Martin even as ever was, there flew into the candle a big moth that had wings, and a'most scared me.

First Citizen

But come to the Duchess, good gossip: what of her?

Mistress Lucy

Marry, it is time you should ask after her, poor lady; she is distraught almost. Why, she has not slept, but paced the chamber all night long. I prayed her to have a posset, or some aqua-vitæ, and to get to bed and sleep a little for her health's sake, but she answered me she was afraid she might dream. That was a strange answer, was it not?

Second Citizen

These great folk have not much sense, so Providence makes it up to them in fine clothes.

Mistress Lucy

    Well, well, God keep murder from us, I say, as long as we are alive.

                                  [*Enter* Lord Moranzone *hurriedly.*]

Moranzone

    Is the Duke dead?

Second Citizen

    He has a knife in his heart, which they say is not healthy for any man.

Moranzone

    Who is accused of having killed him?

Second Citizen

    Why, the prisoner, sir.

Moranzone

    But who is the prisoner?

Second Citizen

    Why, he that is accused of the Duke's murder.

Moranzone

    I mean, what is his name?

Second Citizen

    Faith, the same which his godfathers gave him: what else should it be?

Tipstaff

    Guido Ferranti is his name, my lord.

Moranzone

    I almost knew thine answer ere you gave it.

                                         [*Aside.*]

    Yet it is strange he should have killed the Duke,

Seeing he left me in such different mood.

It is most likely when he saw the man,

This devil who had sold his father's life,

That passion from their seat within his heart

Thrust all his boyish theories of love,

And in their place set vengeance; yet I marvel

That he escaped not.

> [*Turning again to the crowd.*]

How was he taken? Tell me.

Third Citizen

Marry, sir, he was taken by the heels.

Moranzone

But who seized him?

Third Citizen

Why, those that did lay hold of him.

Moranzone

How was the alarm given?

Third Citizen

That I cannot tell you, sir.

Mistress Lucy

It was the Duchess herself who pointed him out.

Moranzone [aside]

The Duchess! There is something strange in this.

Mistress Lucy

Ay! And the dagger was in his hand—the Duchess's own dagger.

Moranzone

What did you say?

Mistress Lucy

Why, marry, that it was with the Duchess's dagger that the Duke was killed.

Moranzone [aside]

There is some mystery about this: I cannot understand it.

Second Citizen

They be very long a-coming,

First Citizen

I warrant they will come soon enough for the prisoner.

Tipstaff

Silence in the Court!

First Citizen

Thou dost break silence in bidding us keep it, Master Tipstaff.

[*Enter the* Lord Justice *and the other Judges.*]

Second Citizen

Who is he in scarlet? Is he the headsman?

Third Citizen

Nay, he is the Lord Justice.

[*Enter* Guido *guarded.*]

Second Citizen

There be the prisoner surely.

Third Citizen

He looks honest.

First Citizen

That be his villany: knaves nowadays do look so honest that honest folk are forced to look like knaves so as to be different.

210

[*Enter the Headman, who takes his stand behind* Guido.]

Second Citizen

Yon be the headsman then! O Lord! Is the axe sharp, think you?

First Citizen

Ay! sharper than thy wits are; but the edge is not towards him, mark you.

Second Citizen [scratching his neck]

I' faith, I like it not so near.

First Citizen

Tut, thou need'st not be afraid; they never cut the heads of common folk: they do but hang us.

[*Trumpets outside.*]

Third Citizen

What are the trumpets for? Is the trial over?

First Citizen

Nay, 'tis for the Duchess.

[*Enter the* Duchess *in black velvet; her train of flowered black velvet is carried by two pages in violet; with her is the* Cardinal *in scarlet, and the gentlemen of the Court in black; she takes her seat on the throne above the Judges, who rise and take their caps off as she enters; the* Cardinal *sits next to her a little lower; the Courtiers group themselves about the throne.*]

Second Citizen

O poor lady, how pale she is! Will she sit there?

First Citizen

Ay! she is in the Duke's place now.

Second Citizen

That is a good thing for Padua; the Duchess is a very kind and merciful Duchess; why, she cured my child of the ague once.

211

Third Citizen

Ay, and has given us bread: do not forget the bread.

A Soldier

Stand back, good people.

Second Citizen

If we be good, why should we stand back?

Tipstaff

Silence in the Court!

Lord Justice

May it please your Grace,

Is it your pleasure we proceed to trial

Of the Duke's murder? [Duchess bows.]

Set the prisoner forth.

What is thy name?

Guido

It matters not, my lord.

Lord Justice

Guido Ferranti is thy name in Padua.

Guido

A man may die as well under that name as any other.

Lord Justice

Thou art not ignorant

What dreadful charge men lay against thee here,

Namely, the treacherous murder of thy Lord,

Simone Gesso, Duke of Padua;

What dost thou say in answer?

Guido

I say nothing.

Lord Justice [rising]

Guido Ferranti—

Moranzone [stepping from the crowd]

Tarry, my Lord Justice.

Lord Justice

Who art thou that bid'st justice tarry, sir?

Moranzone

So be it justice it can go its way;

But if it be not justice—

Lord Justice

Who is this?

Count Bardi

A very noble gentleman, and well known

To the late Duke.

Lord Justice

Sir, thou art come in time

To see the murder of the Duke avenged.

There stands the man who did this heinous thing.

Moranzone

My lord,

I ask again what proof have ye?

Lord Justice [holding up the dagger]

This dagger,

Which from his blood-stained hands, itself all blood,

Last night the soldiers seized: what further proof

Need we indeed?

Moranzone [takes the danger and approaches the Duchess]

Saw I not such a dagger

Hang from your Grace's girdle yesterday?

[*The* Duchess *shudders and makes no answer.*]

Ah! my Lord Justice, may I speak a moment

With this young man, who in such peril stands?

Lord Justice

Ay, willingly, my lord, and may you turn him

To make a full avowal of his guilt.

[Lord Moranzone *goes over to* Guido, *who stands R. and clutches him by the hand.*]

Moranzone [in a low voice]

She did it! Nay, I saw it in her eyes.

Boy, dost thou think I'll let thy father's son

Be by this woman butchered to his death?

Her husband sold your father, and the wife

Would sell the son in turn.

Guido

Lord Moranzone,

I alone did this thing: be satisfied,

My father is avenged.

Lord Justice

Doth he confess?

Guido

My lord, I do confess

That foul unnatural murder has been done.

First Citizen

Why, look at that: he has a pitiful heart, and does not like murder; they will let him go for that.

Lord Justice

Say you no more?

Guido

My lord, I say this also,

That to spill human blood is deadly sin.

Second Citizen

Marry, he should tell that to the headsman: 'tis a good sentiment.

Guido

Lastly, my lord, I do entreat the Court

To give me leave to utter openly

The dreadful secret of this mystery,

And to point out the very guilty one

Who with this dagger last night slew the Duke.

Lord Justice

Thou hast leave to speak.

Duchess [rising]

I say he shall not speak:

What need have we of further evidence?

Was he not taken in the house at night

In Guilt's own bloody livery?

Lord Justice [showing her the statute]

Your Grace

Can read the law.

Duchess [waiving book aside]

Bethink you, my Lord Justice,

Is it not very like that such a one

May, in the presence of the people here,

Utter some slanderous word against my Lord,

Against the city, or the city's honour,

Perchance against myself.

Lord Justice

My liege, the law.

Duchess

He shall not speak, but, with gags in his mouth,

Shall climb the ladder to the bloody block.

Lord Justice

The law, my liege.

Duchess

We are not bound by law,

But with it we bind others.

Moranzone

My Lord Justice,

Thou wilt not suffer this injustice here.

Lord Justice

The Court needs not thy voice, Lord Moranzone.

Madam, it were a precedent most evil

To wrest the law from its appointed course,

For, though the cause be just, yet anarchy

Might on this licence touch these golden scales

And unjust causes unjust victories gain.

Count Bardi

I do not think your Grace can stay the law.

Duchess

Ay, it is well to preach and prate of law:

Methinks, my haughty lords of Padua,

If ye are hurt in pocket or estate,

So much as makes your monstrous revenues

Less by the value of one ferry toll,

Ye do not wait the tedious law's delay

With such sweet patience as ye counsel me.

Count Bardi

Madam, I think you wrong our nobles here.

Duchess

I think I wrong them not. Which of you all

Finding a thief within his house at night,

With some poor chattel thrust into his rags,

Will stop and parley with him? do ye not

Give him unto the officer and his hook

To be dragged gaolwards straightway?

And so now,

Had ye been men, finding this fellow here,

With my Lord's life still hot upon his hands,

Ye would have haled him out into the court,

And struck his head off with an axe.

Guido

O God!

Duchess

Speak, my Lord Justice.

Lord Justice

Your Grace, it cannot be:

The laws of Padua are most certain here:

And by those laws the common murderer even

May with his own lips plead, and make defence.

Duchess

This is no common murderer, Lord Justice,

But a great outlaw, and a most vile traitor,

Taken in open arms against the state.

For he who slays the man who rules a state

Slays the state also, widows every wife,

And makes each child an orphan, and no less

Is to be held a public enemy,

Than if he came with mighty ordonnance,

And all the spears of Venice at his back,

To beat and batter at our city gates—

Nay, is more dangerous to our commonwealth,

For walls and gates, bastions and forts, and things

Whose common elements are wood and stone

May be raised up, but who can raise again

The ruined body of my murdered lord,

And bid it live and laugh?

Maffio

Now by Saint Paul

I do not think that they will let him speak.

Jeppo Vitellozzo

There is much in this, listen.

Duchess

Wherefore now,

Throw ashes on the head of Padua,

With sable banners hang each silent street,

Let every man be clad in solemn black;

But ere we turn to these sad rites of mourning

Let us bethink us of the desperate hand

Which wrought and brought this ruin on our state,

And straightway pack him to that narrow house,

Where no voice is, but with a little dust

Death fills right up the lying mouths of men.

Guido

> Unhand me, knaves! I tell thee, my Lord Justice,
>
> Thou mightst as well bid the untrammelled ocean,
>
> The winter whirlwind, or the Alpine storm,
>
> Not roar their will, as bid me hold my peace!
>
> Ay! though ye put your knives into my throat,
>
> Each grim and gaping wound shall find a tongue,
>
> And cry against you.

Lord Justice

> Sir, this violence
>
> Avails you nothing; for save the tribunal
>
> Give thee a lawful right to open speech,
>
> Naught that thou sayest can be credited.

[*The* Duchess *smiles and* Guido *falls back with a gesture of despair.*]

> Madam, myself, and these wise Justices,
>
> Will with your Grace's sanction now retire
>
> Into another chamber, to decide
>
> Upon this difficult matter of the law,
>
> And search the statutes and the precedents.

Duchess

> Go, my Lord Justice, search the statutes well,
>
> Nor let this brawling traitor have his way.

Moranzone

> Go, my Lord Justice, search thy conscience well,
>
> Nor let a man be sent to death unheard.

220

[*Exit the* Lord Justice *and the Judges.*]

Duchess

Silence, thou evil genius of my life!

Thou com'st between us two a second time;

This time, my lord, I think the turn is mine.

Guido

I shall not die till I have uttered voice.

Duchess

Thou shalt die silent, and thy secret with thee.

Guido

Art thou that Beatrice, Duchess of Padua?

Duchess

I am what thou hast made me; look at me well,

I am thy handiwork.

Maffio

See, is she not

Like that white tigress which we saw at Venice,

Sent by some Indian soldan to the Doge?

Jeppo

Hush! she may hear thy chatter.

Headsman

My young fellow,

I do not know why thou shouldst care to speak,

Seeing my axe is close upon thy neck,

And words of thine will never blunt its edge.

But if thou art so bent upon it, why

Thou mightest plead unto the Churchman yonder:

The common people call him kindly here,

Indeed I know he has a kindly soul.

Guido

This man, whose trade is death, hath courtesies

More than the others.

Headsman

Why, God love you, sir,

I'll do you your last service on this earth.

Guido

My good Lord Cardinal, in a Christian land,

With Lord Christ's face of mercy looking down

From the high seat of Judgment, shall a man

Die unabsolved, unshrived? And if not so,

May I not tell this dreadful tale of sin,

If any sin there be upon my soul?

Duchess

Thou dost but waste thy time.

Cardinal

Alack, my son,

I have no power with the secular arm.

My task begins when justice has been done,

To urge the wavering sinner to repent

And to confess to Holy Church's ear

The dreadful secrets of a sinful mind.

Duchess

> Thou mayest speak to the confessional
>
> Until thy lips grow weary of their tale,
>
> But here thou shalt not speak.

Guido

> My reverend father,
>
> You bring me but cold comfort.

Cardinal

> Nay, my son,
>
> For the great power of our mother Church,
>
> Ends not with this poor bubble of a world,
>
> Of which we are but dust, as Jerome saith,
>
> For if the sinner doth repentant die,
>
> Our prayers and holy masses much avail
>
> To bring the guilty soul from purgatory.

Duchess

> And when in purgatory thou seest my Lord
>
> With that red star of blood upon his heart,
>
> Tell him I sent thee hither.

Guido

> O dear God!

Moranzone

> This is the woman, is it, whom you loved?

Cardinal

Your Grace is very cruel to this man.

Duchess

No more than he was cruel to her Grace.

Cardinal

Yet mercy is the sovereign right of princes.

Duchess

I got no mercy, and I give it not.

He hath changed my heart into a heart of stone,

He hath sown rank nettles in a goodly field,

He hath poisoned the wells of pity in my breast,

He hath withered up all kindness at the root;

My life is as some famine murdered land,

Whence all good things have perished utterly:

I am what he hath made me.

[*The* Duchess *weeps.*]

Jeppo

Is it not strange

That she should so have loved the wicked Duke?

Maffio

It is most strange when women love their lords,

And when they love them not it is most strange.

Jeppo

What a philosopher thou art, Petrucci!

Maffio

Ay! I can bear the ills of other men,

Which is philosophy.

Duchess

They tarry long,

These greybeards and their council; bid them come;

Bid them come quickly, else I think my heart

Will beat itself to bursting: not indeed,

That I here care to live; God knows my life

Is not so full of joy, yet, for all that,

I would not die companionless, or go

Lonely to Hell.

Look, my Lord Cardinal,

Canst thou not see across my forehead here,

In scarlet letters writ, the word Revenge?

Fetch me some water, I will wash it off:

'Twas branded there last night, but in the day-time

I need not wear it, need I, my Lord Cardinal?

Oh, how it sears and burns into my brain:

Give me a knife; not that one, but another,

And I will cut it out.

Cardinal

It is most natural

To be incensed against the murderous hand

That treacherously stabbed your sleeping lord.

Duchess

I would, old Cardinal, I could burn that hand;

But it will burn hereafter.

Cardinal

Nay, the Church

Ordains us to forgive our enemies.

Duchess

Forgiveness? what is that? I never got it.

They come at last: well, my Lord Justice, well.

[*Enter the* Lord Justice.]

Lord Justice

Most gracious Lady, and our sovereign Liege,

We have long pondered on the point at issue,

And much considered of your Grace's wisdom,

And never wisdom spake from fairer lips—

Duchess

Proceed, sir, without compliment.

Lord Justice

We find,

As your own Grace did rightly signify,

That any citizen, who by force or craft

Conspires against the person of the Liege,

Is ipso facto outlaw, void of rights

Such as pertain to other citizens,

Is traitor, and a public enemy,

Who may by any casual sword be slain

Without the slayer's danger; nay, if brought

Into the presence of the tribunal,

Must with dumb lips and silence reverent

Listen unto his well-deserved doom,

Nor has the privilege of open speech.

Duchess

I thank thee, my Lord Justice, heartily;

I like your law: and now I pray dispatch

This public outlaw to his righteous doom;

What is there more?

Lord Justice

Ay, there is more, your Grace.

This man being alien born, not Paduan,

Nor by allegiance bound unto the Duke,

Save such as common nature doth lay down,

Hath, though accused of treasons manifold,

Whose slightest penalty is certain death,

Yet still the right of public utterance

Before the people and the open court;

Nay, shall be much entreated by the Court,

To make some formal pleading for his life,

Lest his own city, righteously incensed,

Should with an unjust trial tax our state,

And wars spring up against the commonwealth:

So merciful are the laws of Padua

Unto the stranger living in her gates.

Duchess

Being of my Lord's household, is he stranger here?

Lord Justice

Ay, until seven years of service spent

He cannot be a Paduan citizen.

Guido

I thank thee, my Lord Justice, heartily;

I like your law.

Second Citizen

I like no law at all:

Were there no law there'd be no law-breakers,

So all men would be virtuous.

First Citizen

So they would;

'Tis a wise saying that, and brings you far.

Tipstaff

Ay! to the gallows, knave.

Duchess

Is this the law?

Lord Justice

It is the law most certainly, my liege.

Duchess

Show me the book: 'tis written in blood-red.

Jeppo

Look at the Duchess.

Duchess

Thou accursed law,

I would that I could tear thee from the state

As easy as I tear thee from this book.

> [*Tears out the page.*]

Come here, Count Bardi: are you honourable?

Get a horse ready for me at my house,

For I must ride to Venice instantly.

Bardi

To Venice, Madam?

Duchess

Not a word of this,

Go, go at once. [Exit Count Bardi.]

A moment, my Lord Justice.

If, as thou sayest it, this is the law—

Nay, nay, I doubt not that thou sayest right,

Though right be wrong in such a case as this—

May I not by the virtue of mine office

Adjourn this court until another day?

Lord Justice

Madam, you cannot stay a trial for blood.

Duchess

I will not tarry then to hear this man

Rail with rude tongue against our sacred person.

Come, gentlemen.

Lord Justice

My liege,

You cannot leave this court until the prisoner

Be purged or guilty of this dread offence.

Duchess

Cannot, Lord Justice? By what right do you

Set barriers in my path where I should go?

Am I not Duchess here in Padua,

And the state's regent?

Lord Justice

For that reason, Madam,

Being the fountain-head of life and death

Whence, like a mighty river, justice flows,

Without thy presence justice is dried up

And fails of purpose: thou must tarry here.

Duchess

What, wilt thou keep me here against my will?

Lord Justice

We pray thy will be not against the law.

Duchess

What if I force my way out of the court?

Lord Justice

Thou canst not force the Court to give thee way.

Duchess

I will not tarry. [Rises from her seat.]

Lord Justice

Is the usher here?

Let him stand forth. [Usher comes forward.]

Thou knowest thy business, sir.

[*The Usher closes the doors of the court, which are L., and when the* Duchess *and her retinue approach, kneels down.*]

Usher

In all humility I beseech your Grace

Turn not my duty to discourtesy,

Nor make my unwelcome office an offence.

Duchess

Is there no gentleman amongst you all

To prick this prating fellow from our way?

Maffio [drawing his sword]

Ay! that will I.

Lord Justice

Count Maffio, have a care,

And you, sir. [To Jeppo.]

The first man who draws his sword

Upon the meanest officer of this Court,

Dies before nightfall.

Duchess

Sirs, put up your swords:

It is most meet that I should hear this man.

[*Goes back to throne.*]

Moranzone

    Now hast thou got thy enemy in thy hand.

Lord Justice [taking the time-glass up]

    Guido Ferranti, while the crumbling sand

    Falls through this time-glass, thou hast leave to speak.

    This and no more.

Guido

    It is enough, my lord.

Lord Justice

    Thou standest on the extreme verge of death;

    See that thou speakest nothing but the truth,

    Naught else will serve thee.

Guido

    If I speak it not,

    Then give my body to the headsman there.

Lord Justice [turns the time-glass]

    Let there be silence while the prisoner speaks.

Tipstaff

    Silence in the Court there.

Guido

    My Lords Justices,

    And reverent judges of this worthy court,

    I hardly know where to begin my tale,

    So strangely dreadful is this history.

First, let me tell you of what birth I am.

I am the son of that good Duke Lorenzo

Who was with damned treachery done to death

By a most wicked villain, lately Duke

Of this good town of Padua.

Lord Justice

Have a care,

It will avail thee nought to mock this prince

Who now lies in his coffin.

Maffio

By Saint James,

This is the Duke of Parma's rightful heir.

Jeppo

I always thought him noble.

Guido

I confess

That with the purport of a just revenge,

A most just vengeance on a man of blood,

I entered the Duke's household, served his will,

Sat at his board, drank of his wine, and was

His intimate: so much I will confess,

And this too, that I waited till he grew

To give the fondest secrets of his life

Into my keeping, till he fawned on me,

And trusted me in every private matter

Even as my noble father trusted him;

That for this thing I waited.

[*To the Headsman.*]

Thou man of blood!

Turn not thine axe on me before the time:

Who knows if it be time for me to die?

Is there no other neck in court but mine?

Lord Justice

The sand within the time-glass flows apace.

Come quickly to the murder of the Duke.

Guido

I will be brief: Last night at twelve o' the clock,

By a strong rope I scaled the palace wall,

With purport to revenge my father's murder—

Ay! with that purport I confess, my lord.

This much I will acknowledge, and this also,

That as with stealthy feet I climbed the stair

Which led unto the chamber of the Duke,

And reached my hand out for the scarlet cloth

Which shook and shivered in the gusty door,

Lo! the white moon that sailed in the great heaven

Flooded with silver light the darkened room,

Night lit her candles for me, and I saw

The man I hated, cursing in his sleep;

And thinking of a most dear father murdered,

Sold to the scaffold, bartered to the block,

I smote the treacherous villain to the heart

With this same dagger, which by chance I found

Within the chamber.

Duchess [rising from her seat]

Oh!

Guido [hurriedly]

I killed the Duke.

Now, my Lord Justice, if I may crave a boon,

Suffer me not to see another sun

Light up the misery of this loathsome world.

Lord Justice

Thy boon is granted, thou shalt die to-night.

Lead him away. Come, Madam

[Guido is led off; as he goes the Duchess stretches out her arms and rushes down the stage.]

Duchess

Guido! Guido!

[*Faints.*]

Tableau

END OF ACT IV.

ACT V

SCENE

A dungeon in the public prison of Padua; Guido lies asleep on a pallet (L.C.); a table with a goblet on it is set (L.C.); five soldiers are drinking and playing dice in the corner on a stone table; one of them has a lantern hung to his halbert; a torch is set in the wall over Guido's head. Two grated windows behind, one on each side of the door which is (C.), look out into the passage; the stage is rather dark.

First Soldier [throws dice]

> Sixes again! good Pietro.

Second Soldier

> I' faith, lieutenant, I will play with thee no more. I will lose everything.

Third Soldier

> Except thy wits; thou art safe there!

Second Soldier

> Ay, ay, he cannot take them from me.

Third Soldier

> No; for thou hast no wits to give him.

The Soldiers [loudly]

> Ha! ha! ha!

First Soldier

> Silence! You will wake the prisoner; he is asleep.

Second Soldier

> What matter? He will get sleep enough when he is buried. I warrant he'd be glad if we could wake him when he's in the grave.

Third Soldier

Nay! for when he wakes there it will be judgment day.

Second Soldier

Ay, and he has done a grievous thing; for, look you, to murder one of us who are but flesh and blood is a sin, and to kill a Duke goes being near against the law.

First Soldier

Well, well, he was a wicked Duke.

Second Soldier

And so he should not have touched him; if one meddles with wicked people, one is like to be tainted with their wickedness.

Third Soldier

Ay, that is true. How old is the prisoner?

Second Soldier

Old enough to do wrong, and not old enough to be wise.

First Soldier

Why, then, he might be any age.

Second Soldier

They say the Duchess wanted to pardon him.

First Soldier

Is that so?

Second Soldier

Ay, and did much entreat the Lord Justice, but he would not.

First Soldier

I had thought, Pietro, that the Duchess was omnipotent.

Second Soldier

True, she is well-favoured; I know none so comely.

The Soldiers

Ha! ha! ha!

First Soldier

I meant I had thought our Duchess could do anything.

Second Soldier

Nay, for he is now given over to the Justices, and they will see that justice be done; they and stout Hugh the headsman; but when his head is off, why then the Duchess can pardon him if she likes; there is no law against that.

First Soldier

I do not think that stout Hugh, as you call him, will do the business for him after all. This Guido is of gentle birth, and so by the law can drink poison first, if it so be his pleasure.

Third Soldier

And if he does not drink it?

First Soldier

Why, then, they will kill him.

[*Knocking comes at the door.*]

First Soldier

See who that is.

[*Third Soldier goes over and looks through the wicket.*]

Third Soldier

It is a woman, sir.

First Soldier

Is she pretty?

Third Soldier

I can't tell. She is masked, lieutenant.

First Soldier

It is only very ugly or very beautiful women who ever hide their faces. Let her in.

[*Soldier opens the door, and the* Duchess *masked and cloaked enters.*]

Duchess [to Third Soldier]

Are you the officer on guard?

First Soldier [coming forward]

I am, madam.

Duchess

I must see the prisoner alone.

First Soldier

I am afraid that is impossible. [The Duchess hands him a ring, he looks at and returns it to her with a bow and makes a sign to the Soldiers.] Stand without there.

[*Exeunt the Soldiers.*]

Duchess

Officer, your men are somewhat rough.

First Soldier

They mean no harm.

Duchess

I shall be going back in a few minutes. As I pass through the corridor do not let them try and lift my mask.

First Soldier

You need not be afraid, madam.

Duchess

I have a particular reason for wishing my face not to be seen.

First Soldier

Madam, with this ring you can go in and out as you please; it is the

Duchess's own ring.

Duchess

Leave us. [The Soldier turns to go out.] A moment, sir. For what hour is . . .

First Soldier

At twelve o'clock, madam, we have orders to lead him out; but I dare say he won't wait for us; he's more like to take a drink out of that poison yonder. Men are afraid of the headsman.

Duchess

Is that poison?

First Soldier

Ay, madam, and very sure poison too.

Duchess

You may go, sir.

First Soldier

By Saint James, a pretty hand! I wonder who she is. Some woman who loved him, perhaps.

[*Exit.*]

Duchess [taking her mark off]

At last!

He can escape now in this cloak and vizard,

We are of a height almost: they will not know him;

As for myself what matter?

So that he does not curse me as he goes,

I care but little: I wonder will he curse me.

He has the right. It is eleven now;

They will not come till twelve.

[Goes over to the table.]

So this is poison.

Is it not strange that in this liquor here

There lies the key to all philosophies?

[Takes the cup up.]

It smells of poppies. I remember well

That, when I was a child in Sicily,

I took the scarlet poppies from the corn,

And made a little wreath, and my grave uncle,

Don John of Naples, laughed: I did not know

That they had power to stay the springs of life,

To make the pulse cease beating, and to chill

The blood in its own vessels, till men come

And with a hook hale the poor body out,

And throw it in a ditch: the body, ay,—

What of the soul? that goes to heaven or hell.

Where will mine go?

   [Takes the torch from the wall, and goes over to the bed.]

How peacefully here he sleeps,

Like a young schoolboy tired out with play:

I would that I could sleep so peacefully,

But I have dreams. [Bending over him.]

Poor boy: what if I kissed him?

No, no, my lips would burn him like a fire.

He has had enough of Love. Still that white neck

Will 'scape the headsman: I have seen to that:

He will get hence from Padua to-night,

And that is well. You are very wise, Lord Justices,

And yet you are not half so wise as I am,

And that is well.

O God! how I have loved you,

And what a bloody flower did Love bear!

[*Comes back to the table.*]

What if I drank these juices, and so ceased?

Were it not better than to wait till Death

Come to my bed with all his serving men,

Remorse, disease, old age, and misery?

I wonder does one suffer much: I think

That I am very young to die like this,

But so it must be. Why, why should I die?

He will escape to-night, and so his blood

Will not be on my head. No, I must die;

I have been guilty, therefore I must die;

He loves me not, and therefore I must die:

I would die happier if he would kiss me,

But he will not do that. I did not know him.

I thought he meant to sell me to the Judge;

That is not strange; we women never know

Our lovers till they leave us.

> [*Bell begins to toll.*]

Thou vile bell,

That like a bloodhound from thy brazen throat

Call'st for this man's life, cease! thou shalt not get it.

He stirs—I must be quick: [Takes up cup.]

O Love, Love, Love,

I did not think that I would pledge thee thus!

[*Drinks poison, and sets the cup down on the table behind her: the noise wakens* Guido, *who starts up, and does not see what she has done. There is silence for a minute, each looking at the other.*]

I do not come to ask your pardon now,

Seeing I know I stand beyond all pardon;

Enough of that: I have already, sir,

Confessed my sin to the Lords Justices;

They would not listen to me: and some said

I did invent a tale to save your life;

You have trafficked with me; others said

That women played with pity as with men;

Others that grief for my slain Lord and husband

Had robbed me of my wits: they would not hear me,

And, when I sware it on the holy book,

They bade the doctor cure me. They are ten,

Ten against one, and they possess your life.

They call me Duchess here in Padua.

I do not know, sir; if I be the Duchess,

I wrote your pardon, and they would not take it;

They call it treason, say I taught them that;

Maybe I did. Within an hour, Guido,

They will be here, and drag you from the cell,

And bind your hands behind your back, and bid you

Kneel at the block: I am before them there;

Here is the signet ring of Padua,

'Twill bring you safely through the men on guard;

There is my cloak and vizard; they have orders

Not to be curious: when you pass the gate

Turn to the left, and at the second bridge

You will find horses waiting: by to-morrow

You will be at Venice, safe. [A pause.]

Do you not speak?

Will you not even curse me ere you go?—

You have the right. [A pause.]

You do not understand

There lies between you and the headsman's axe

Hardly so much sand in the hour-glass

As a child's palm could carry: here is the ring:

I have washed my hand: there is no blood upon it:

244

You need not fear. Will you not take the ring?

Guido [takes ring and kisses it]

> Ay! gladly, Madam.

Duchess

> And leave Padua.

Guido

> Leave Padua.

Duchess

> But it must be to-night.

Guido

> To-night it shall be.

Duchess

> Oh, thank God for that!

Guido

> So I can live; life never seemed so sweet

> As at this moment.

Duchess

> Do not tarry, Guido,

> There is my cloak: the horse is at the bridge,

> The second bridge below the ferry house:

> Why do you tarry? Can your ears not hear

> This dreadful bell, whose every ringing stroke

> Robs one brief minute from your boyish life.

> Go quickly.

Guido

Ay! he will come soon enough.

Duchess

Who?

Guido [calmly]

Why, the headsman.

Duchess

No, no.

Guido

Only he

Can bring me out of Padua.

Duchess

You dare not!

You dare not burden my o'erburdened soul

With two dead men! I think one is enough.

For when I stand before God, face to face,

I would not have you, with a scarlet thread

Around your white throat, coming up behind

To say I did it.

Guido

Madam, I wait.

Duchess

No, no, you cannot: you do not understand,

I have less power in Padua to-night

Than any common woman; they will kill you.

I saw the scaffold as I crossed the square,

246

Already the low rabble throng about it

With fearful jests, and horrid merriment,

As though it were a morris-dancer's platform,

And not Death's sable throne. O Guido, Guido,

You must escape!

Guido

Madam, I tarry here.

Duchess

Guido, you shall not: it would be a thing

So terrible that the amazed stars

Would fall from heaven, and the palsied moon

Be in her sphere eclipsed, and the great sun

Refuse to shine upon the unjust earth

Which saw thee die.

Guido

Be sure I shall not stir.

Duchess [wringing her hands]

Is one sin not enough, but must it breed

A second sin more horrible again

Than was the one that bare it? O God, God,

Seal up sin's teeming womb, and make it barren,

I will not have more blood upon my hand

Than I have now.

Guido [seizing her hand]

What! am I fallen so low

That I may not have leave to die for you?

Duchess [tearing her hand away]

Die for me?—no, my life is a vile thing,

Thrown to the miry highways of this world;

You shall not die for me, you shall not, Guido;

I am a guilty woman.

Guido

Guilty?—let those

Who know what a thing temptation is,

Let those who have not walked as we have done,

In the red fire of passion, those whose lives

Are dull and colourless, in a word let those,

If any such there be, who have not loved,

Cast stones against you. As for me—

Duchess

Alas!

Guido [falling at her feet]

You are my lady, and you are my love!

O hair of gold, O crimson lips, O face

Made for the luring and the love of man!

Incarnate image of pure loveliness!

Worshipping thee I do forget the past,

Worshipping thee my soul comes close to thine,

Worshipping thee I seem to be a god,

And though they give my body to the block,

Yet is my love eternal!

[Duchess *puts her hands over her face:* Guido *draws them down.*]

    Sweet, lift up

The trailing curtains that overhang your eyes

That I may look into those eyes, and tell you

I love you, never more than now when Death

Thrusts his cold lips between us: Beatrice,

I love you: have you no word left to say?

Oh, I can bear the executioner,

But not this silence: will you not say you love me?

Speak but that word and Death shall lose his sting,

But speak it not, and fifty thousand deaths

Are, in comparison, mercy. Oh, you are cruel,

And do not love me.

Duchess

    Alas! I have no right

For I have stained the innocent hands of love

With spilt-out blood: there is blood on the ground;

I set it there.

Guido

    Sweet, it was not yourself,

It was some devil tempted you.

Duchess [rising suddenly]

No, no,

We are each our own devil, and we make

This world our hell.

Guido

Then let high Paradise

Fall into Tartarus! for I shall make

This world my heaven for a little space.

The sin was mine, if any sin there was.

'Twas I who nurtured murder in my heart,

Sweetened my meats, seasoned my wine with it,

And in my fancy slew the accursed Duke

A hundred times a day. Why, had this man

Died half so often as I wished him to,

Death had been stalking ever through the house,

And murder had not slept.

But you, fond heart,

Whose little eyes grew tender over a whipt hound,

You whom the little children laughed to see

Because you brought the sunlight where you passed,

You the white angel of God's purity,

This which men call your sin, what was it?

Duchess

Ay!

What was it? There are times it seems a dream,

An evil dream sent by an evil god,

And then I see the dead face in the coffin

And know it is no dream, but that my hand

Is red with blood, and that my desperate soul

Striving to find some haven for its love

From the wild tempest of this raging world,

Has wrecked its bark upon the rocks of sin.

What was it, said you?—murder merely? Nothing

But murder, horrible murder.

Guido

Nay, nay, nay,

'Twas but the passion-flower of your love

That in one moment leapt to terrible life,

And in one moment bare this gory fruit,

Which I had plucked in thought a thousand times.

My soul was murderous, but my hand refused;

Your hand wrought murder, but your soul was pure.

And so I love you, Beatrice, and let him

Who has no mercy for your stricken head,

Lack mercy up in heaven! Kiss me, sweet.

[Tries to kiss her.]

Duchess

No, no, your lips are pure, and mine are soiled,

For Guilt has been my paramour, and Sin

251

Lain in my bed: O Guido, if you love me

Get hence, for every moment is a worm

Which gnaws your life away: nay, sweet, get hence,

And if in after time you think of me,

Think of me as of one who loved you more

Than anything on earth; think of me, Guido,

As of a woman merely, one who tried

To make her life a sacrifice to love,

And slew love in the trial: Oh, what is that?

The bell has stopped from ringing, and I hear

The feet of armed men upon the stair.

Guido [aside]

That is the signal for the guard to come.

Duchess

Why has the bell stopped ringing?

Guido

If you must know,

That stops my life on this side of the grave,

But on the other we shall meet again.

Duchess

No, no, 'tis not too late: you must get hence;

The horse is by the bridge, there is still time.

Away, away, you must not tarry here!

[*Noise of Soldiers in the passage.*]

A Voice Outside

Room for the Lord Justice of Padua!

[*The* Lord Justice *is seen through the grated window passing down the corridor preceded by men bearing torches.*]

Duchess

It is too late.

A Voice Outside

Room for the headsman.

Duchess [sinks down]

Oh!

[*The Headsman with his axe on his shoulder is seen passing the corridor, followed by Monks bearing candles.*]

Guido

Farewell, dear love, for I must drink this poison.

I do not fear the headsman, but I would die

Not on the lonely scaffold.

But here,

Here in thine arms, kissing thy mouth: farewell!

[*Goes to the table and takes the goblet up.*]

What, art thou empty?

[*Throws it to the ground.*]

O thou churlish gaoler,

Even of poisons niggard!

Duchess [faintly]

Blame him not.

Guido

O God! you have not drunk it, Beatrice?

Tell me you have not?

Duchess

Were I to deny it,

There is a fire eating at my heart

Which would find utterance.

Guido

O treacherous love,

Why have you not left a drop for me?

Duchess

No, no, it held but death enough for one.

Guido

Is there no poison still upon your lips,

That I may draw it from them?

Duchess

Why should you die?

You have not spilt blood, and so need not die:

I have spilt blood, and therefore I must die.

Was it not said blood should be spilt for blood?

Who said that? I forget.

Guido

Tarry for me,

Our souls will go together.

Duchess

Nay, you must live.

There are many other women in the world

Who will love you, and not murder for your sake.

Guido

I love you only.

Duchess

You need not die for that.

Guido

Ah, if we die together, love, why then

Can we not lie together in one grave?

Duchess

A grave is but a narrow wedding-bed.

Guido

It is enough for us

Duchess

And they will strew it

With a stark winding-sheet, and bitter herbs:

I think there are no roses in the grave,

Or if there are, they all are withered now

Since my Lord went there.

Guido

Ah! dear Beatrice,

Your lips are roses that death cannot wither.

Duchess

Nay, if we lie together, will not my lips

Fall into dust, and your enamoured eyes

Shrivel to sightless sockets, and the worms,

Which are our groomsmen, eat away your heart?

Guido

I do not care: Death has no power on love.

And so by Love's immortal sovereignty

I will die with you.

Duchess

But the grave is black,

And the pit black, so I must go before

To light the candles for your coming hither.

No, no, I will not die, I will not die.

Love, you are strong, and young, and very brave;

Stand between me and the angel of death,

And wrestle with him for me.

[*Thrusts* Guido *in front of her with his back to the audience.*]

I will kiss you,

When you have thrown him. Oh, have you no cordial,

To stay the workings of this poison in me?

Are there no rivers left in Italy

That you will not fetch me one cup of water

To quench this fire?

Guido

O God!

Duchess

> You did not tell me
>
> There was a drought in Italy, and no water:
>
> Nothing but fire.

Guido

> O Love!

Duchess

> Send for a leech,
>
> Not him who stanched my husband, but another
>
> We have no time: send for a leech, I say:
>
> There is an antidote against each poison,
>
> And he will sell it if we give him money.
>
> Tell him that I will give him Padua,
>
> For one short hour of life: I will not die.
>
> Oh, I am sick to death; no, do not touch me,
>
> This poison gnaws my heart: I did not know
>
> It was such pain to die: I thought that life
>
> Had taken all the agonies to itself;
>
> It seems it is not so.

Guido

> O damnéd stars
>
> Quench your vile cresset-lights in tears, and bid
>
> The moon, your mistress, shine no more to-night.

Duchess

> Guido, why are we here? I think this room

Is poorly furnished for a marriage chamber.

Let us get hence at once. Where are the horses?

We should be on our way to Venice now.

How cold the night is! We must ride faster.

[*The Monks begin to chant outside.*]

Music! It should be merrier; but grief

Is of the fashion now—I know not why.

You must not weep: do we not love each other?—

That is enough. Death, what do you here?

You were not bidden to this table, sir;

Away, we have no need of you: I tell you

It was in wine I pledged you, not in poison.

They lied who told you that I drank your poison.

It was spilt upon the ground, like my Lord's blood;

You came too late.

Guido

Sweet, there is nothing there:

These things are only unreal shadows.

Duchess

Death,

Why do you tarry, get to the upper chamber;

The cold meats of my husband's funeral feast

Are set for you; this is a wedding feast.

You are out of place, sir; and, besides, 'tis summer.

We do not need these heavy fires now,

You scorch us.

Oh, I am burned up,

Can you do nothing? Water, give me water,

Or else more poison. No: I feel no pain—

Is it not curious I should feel no pain?—

And Death has gone away, I am glad of that.

I thought he meant to part us. Tell me, Guido,

Are you not sorry that you ever saw me?

Guido

I swear I would not have lived otherwise.

Why, in this dull and common world of ours

Men have died looking for such moments as this

And have not found them.

Duchess

Then you are not sorry?

How strange that seems.

Guido

What, Beatrice, have I not

Stood face to face with beauty? That is enough

For one man's life. Why, love, I could be merry;

I have been often sadder at a feast,

But who were sad at such a feast as this

When Love and Death are both our cup-bearers?

We love and die together.

Duchess

Oh, I have been

Guilty beyond all women, and indeed

Beyond all women punished. Do you think—

No, that could not be—Oh, do you think that love

Can wipe the bloody stain from off my hands,

Pour balm into my wounds, heal up my hurts,

And wash my scarlet sins as white as snow?—

For I have sinned.

Guido

They do not sin at all

Who sin for love.

Duchess

No, I have sinned, and yet

Perchance my sin will be forgiven me.

I have loved much

[*They kiss each other now for the first time in this Act, when suddenly the* Duchess *leaps up in the dreadful spasm of death, tears in agony at her dress, and finally, with face twisted and distorted with pain, falls back dead in a chair.* Guido *seizing her dagger from her belt, kills himself; and, as he falls across her knees, clutches at the cloak which is on the back of the chair, and throws it entirely over her. There is a little pause. Then down the passage comes the tramp of Soldiers; the door is opened, and the* Lord Justice, *the* Headsman, *and the* Guard *enter and see this figure shrouded in black, and* Guido *lying dead across her. The* Lord Justice *rushes forward and drags the cloak off the* Duchess, *whose face is now the marble image of peace, the sign of God's forgiveness.*]

Tableau

CURTAI

About Author

Oscar Fingal O'Flahertie Wills Wilde (16 October 1854 – 30 November 1900) was an Irish poet and playwright. After writing in different forms throughout the 1880s, the early 1890s saw him become one of the most popular playwrights in London. He is best remembered for his epigrams and plays, his novel The Picture of Dorian Gray, and the circumstances of his criminal conviction for "gross indecency", imprisonment, and early death at age 46.

Wilde's parents were successful Anglo-Irish intellectuals in Dublin. A young Wilde learned to speak fluent French and German. At university, Wilde read Greats; he demonstrated himself to be an exceptional classicist, first at Trinity College Dublin, then at Oxford. He became associated with the emerging philosophy of aestheticism, led by two of his tutors, Walter Pater and John Ruskin. After university, Wilde moved to London into fashionable cultural and social circles.

As a spokesman for aestheticism, he tried his hand at various literary activities: he published a book of poems, lectured in the United States and Canada on the new "English Renaissance in Art" and interior decoration, and then returned to London where he worked prolifically as a journalist. Known for his biting wit, flamboyant dress and glittering conversational skill, Wilde became one of the best-known personalities of his day. At the turn of the 1890s, he refined his ideas about the supremacy of art in a series of dialogues and essays, and incorporated themes of decadence, duplicity, and beauty into what would be his only novel, The Picture of Dorian Gray (1890). The opportunity to construct aesthetic details precisely, and combine them with larger social themes, drew Wilde to write drama. He wrote Salome (1891) in French while in Paris but it was refused a licence for England due to an absolute prohibition on the portrayal of Biblical subjects on the English stage. Unperturbed, Wilde produced four society comedies in the early 1890s, which made him one of the most successful playwrights of late-Victorian London.

At the height of his fame and success, while The Importance of Being Earnest (1895) was still being performed in London, Wilde had the Marquess of Queensberry prosecuted for criminal libel. The Marquess was the father of Wilde's lover, Lord Alfred Douglas. The libel trial unearthed evidence that caused Wilde to drop his charges and led to his own arrest and trial for gross indecency with men. After two more trials he was convicted and sentenced to two years' hard labour, the maximum penalty, and was jailed from 1895 to 1897. During his last year in prison, he wrote De Profundis (published posthumously in 1905), a long letter which discusses his spiritual journey through his trials, forming a dark counterpoint to his earlier philosophy of pleasure. On his release, he left immediately for France, never to return to Ireland or Britain. There he wrote his last work, The Ballad of Reading Gaol (1898), a long poem commemorating the harsh rhythms of prison life.

Early life

Oscar Wilde was born at 21 Westland Row, Dublin (now home of the Oscar Wilde Centre, Trinity College), the second of three children born to Anglo-Irish Sir William Wilde and Jane Wilde, two years behind his brother William ("Willie"). Wilde's mother had distant Italian ancestry,and under the pseudonym "Speranza" (the Italian word for 'hope'), wrote poetry for the revolutionary Young Irelanders in 1848; she was a lifelong Irish nationalist. She read the Young Irelanders' poetry to Oscar and Willie, inculcating a love of these poets in her sons. Lady Wilde's interest in the neo-classical revival showed in the paintings and busts of ancient Greece and Rome in her home.

William Wilde was Ireland's leading oto-ophthalmologic (ear and eye) surgeon and was knighted in 1864 for his services as medical adviser and assistant commissioner to the censuses of Ireland. He also wrote books about Irish archaeology and peasant folklore. A renowned philanthropist, his dispensary for the care of the city's poor at the rear of Trinity College, Dublin, was the forerunner of the Dublin Eye and Ear Hospital, now located at Adelaide Road. On his father's side Wilde was descended from a Dutchman, Colonel de Wilde, who went to Ireland with King William of Orange's invading army in 1690, and numerous Anglo-Irish ancestors. On his mother's side, Wilde's ancestors included a bricklayer from County Durham, who emigrated to Ireland sometime in the 1770s.

Wilde was baptised as an infant in St. Mark's Church, Dublin, the local Church of Ireland (Anglican) church. When the church was closed, the records were moved to the nearby St. Ann's Church, Dawson Street. Davis Coakley mentions a second baptism by a Catholic priest, Father Prideaux Fox, who befriended Oscar's mother circa 1859. According to Fox's testimony in Donahoe's Magazine in 1905, Jane Wilde would visit his chapel in Glencree, County Wicklow, for Mass and would take her sons with her. She asked Father Fox in this period to baptise her sons.

Fox described it in this way:

"I am not sure if she ever became a Catholic herself but it was not long before she asked me to instruct two of her children, one of them being the future erratic genius, Oscar Wilde. After a few weeks I baptized these two children, Lady Wilde herself being present on the occasion.

In addition to his children with his wife, Sir William Wilde was the father of three children born out of wedlock before his marriage: Henry Wilson, born in 1838 to one woman, and Emily and Mary Wilde, born in 1847 and 1849, respectively, to a second woman. Sir William acknowledged paternity of his illegitimate or "natural" children and provided for their education, arranging for them to be reared by his relatives rather than with his legitimate children in his family household with his wife.

In 1855, the family moved to No. 1 Merrion Square, where Wilde's sister, Isola, was born in 1857. The Wildes' new home was larger. With both his parents' success and delight in social life, the house soon became the site of a "unique medical and cultural milieu". Guests at their salon included Sheridan Le Fanu, Charles Lever, George Petrie, Isaac Butt, William Rowan Hamilton and Samuel Ferguson.

Until he was nine, Oscar Wilde was educated at home, where a French nursemaid and a German governess taught him their languages. He attended Portora Royal School in Enniskillen, County Fermanagh, from 1864 to 1871. Until his early twenties, Wilde summered at the villa, Moytura House, which his father had built in Cong, County Mayo. There the young Wilde and his brother Willie played with George Moore.

Isola died at age nine of meningitis. Wilde's poem "Requiescat" is written to her memory.

"Tread lightly, she is near

Under the snow

Speak gently, she can hear

the daisies grow"

University education: 1870s

Trinity College, Dublin

Wilde left Portora with a royal scholarship to read classics at Trinity College, Dublin, from 1871 to 1874, sharing rooms with his older brother Willie Wilde. Trinity, one of the leading classical schools, placed him with scholars such as R. Y. Tyrell, Arthur Palmer, Edward Dowden and his tutor, Professor J. P. Mahaffy, who inspired his interest in Greek literature. As a student Wilde worked with Mahaffy on the latter's book Social Life in Greece. Wilde, despite later reservations, called Mahaffy "my first and best teacher" and "the scholar who showed me how to love Greek things".For his part, Mahaffy boasted of having created Wilde; later, he said Wilde was "the only blot on my tutorship".

The University Philosophical Society also provided an education, as members discussed intellectual and artistic subjects such as Dante Gabriel Rossetti and Algernon Charles Swinburne weekly. Wilde quickly became an established member – the members' suggestion book for 1874 contains two pages of banter (sportingly) mocking Wilde's emergent aestheticism. He presented a paper titled "Aesthetic Morality". At Trinity, Wilde established himself as an outstanding student: he came first in his class in his first year, won a scholarship by competitive examination in his second and, in his finals, won the Berkeley Gold Medal in Greek, the University's highest academic award. He was encouraged to compete for a demyship to Magdalen College, Oxford – which he won easily, having already studied Greek for over nine years.

Magdalen College, Oxford

At Magdalen, he read Greats from 1874 to 1878, and from there he applied to join the Oxford Union, but failed to be elected.

Attracted by its dress, secrecy, and ritual, Wilde petitioned the Apollo Masonic Lodge at Oxford, and was soon raised to the "Sublime Degree of Master Mason".During a resurgent interest in Freemasonry in his third year, he commented he "would be awfully sorry to give it up if I secede from the Protestant Heresy". Wilde's active involvement in Freemasonry lasted only for the time he spent at Oxford; he allowed his membership of the Apollo University Lodge to lapse after failing to pay subscriptions.

Catholicism deeply appealed to him, especially its rich liturgy, and he discussed converting to it with clergy several times. In 1877, Wilde was left speechless after an audience with Pope Pius IX in Rome.He eagerly read the books of Cardinal Newman, a noted Anglican priest who had converted to Catholicism and risen in the church hierarchy. He became more serious in 1878, when he met the Reverend Sebastian Bowden, a priest in the Brompton Oratory who had received some high-profile converts. Neither his father, who threatened to cut off his funds, nor Mahaffy thought much of the plan; but mostly Wilde, the supreme individualist, balked at the last minute from pledging himself to any formal creed. On the appointed day of his baptism, Wilde sent Father Bowden a bunch of altar lilies instead. Wilde did retain a lifelong interest in Catholic theology and liturgy.

While at Magdalen College, Wilde became particularly well known for his role in the aesthetic and decadent movements. He wore his hair long, openly scorned "manly" sports though he occasionally boxed, and he decorated his rooms with peacock feathers, lilies, sunflowers, blue china and other objets d'art. He once remarked to friends, whom he entertained lavishly, "I find it harder and harder every day to live up to my blue china." The line quickly became famous, accepted as a slogan by aesthetes but used against them by critics who sensed in it a terrible vacuousness. Some elements disdained the aesthetes, but their languishing attitudes and showy costumes became a recognised pose. Wilde was once physically attacked by a group of

267

four fellow students, and dealt with them single-handedly, surprising critics. By his third year Wilde had truly begun to develop himself and his myth, and considered his learning to be more expansive than what was within the prescribed texts. This attitude resulted in his being rusticated for one term, after he had returned late to a college term from a trip to Greece with Mahaffy.

Wilde did not meet Walter Pater until his third year, but had been enthralled by his Studies in the History of the Renaissance, published during Wilde's final year in Trinity. Pater argued that man's sensibility to beauty should be refined above all else, and that each moment should be felt to its fullest extent. Years later, in De Profundis, Wilde described Pater's Studies... as "that book that has had such a strange influence over my life".He learned tracts of the book by heart, and carried it with him on travels in later years. Pater gave Wilde his sense of almost flippant devotion to art, though he gained a purpose for it through the lectures and writings of critic John Ruskin. Ruskin despaired at the self-validating aestheticism of Pater, arguing that the importance of art lies in its potential for the betterment of society. Ruskin admired beauty, but believed it must be allied with, and applied to, moral good. When Wilde eagerly attended Ruskin's lecture series The Aesthetic and Mathematic Schools of Art in Florence, he learned about aesthetics as the non-mathematical elements of painting. Despite being given to neither early rising nor manual labour, Wilde volunteered for Ruskin's project to convert a swampy country lane into a smart road neatly edged with flowers.

Wilde won the 1878 Newdigate Prize for his poem "Ravenna", which reflected on his visit there the year before, and he duly read it at Encaenia. In November 1878, he graduated with a double first in his B.A. of Classical Moderations and Literae Humaniores (Greats). Wilde wrote to a friend, "The dons are 'astonied' beyond words – the Bad Boy doing so well in the end!"

Apprenticeship of an aesthete: 1880s

Debut in society

After graduation from Oxford, Wilde returned to Dublin, where he met again Florence Balcombe, a childhood sweetheart. She became engaged to Bram Stoker and they married in 1878. Wilde was disappointed but stoic:

he wrote to her, remembering "the two sweet years – the sweetest years of all my youth" during which they had been close. He also stated his intention to "return to England, probably for good." This he did in 1878, only briefly visiting Ireland twice after that.

Unsure of his next step, Wilde wrote to various acquaintances enquiring about Classics positions at Oxford or Cambridge. The Rise of Historical Criticism was his submission for the Chancellor's Essay prize of 1879, which, though no longer a student, he was still eligible to enter. Its subject, "Historical Criticism among the Ancients" seemed ready-made for Wilde – with both his skill in composition and ancient learning – but he struggled to find his voice with the long, flat, scholarly style. Unusually, no prize was awarded that year.

With the last of his inheritance from the sale of his father's houses, he set himself up as a bachelor in London. The 1881 British Census listed Wilde as a boarder at 1 (now 44) Tite Street, Chelsea, where Frank Miles, a society painter, was the head of the household. Wilde spent the next six years in London and Paris, and in the United States, where he travelled to deliver lectures.

He had been publishing lyrics and poems in magazines since entering Trinity College, especially in Kottabos and the Dublin University Magazine. In mid-1881, at 27 years old, he published Poems, which collected, revised and expanded his poems.

The book was generally well received, and sold out its first print run of 750 copies. Punch was less enthusiastic, saying "The poet is Wilde, but his poetry's tame". By a tight vote, the Oxford Union condemned the book for alleged plagiarism. The librarian, who had requested the book for the library, returned the presentation copy to Wilde with a note of apology.Biographer Richard Ellmann argues that Wilde's poem "Hélas!" was a sincere, though flamboyant, attempt to explain the dichotomies the poet saw in himself; one line reads: "To drift with every passion till my soul

Is a stringed lute on which all winds can play".

The book had further printings in 1882. It was bound in a rich, enamel parchment cover (embossed with gilt blossom) and printed on hand-made Dutch paper; over the next few years, Wilde presented many copies to the dignitaries and writers who received him during his lecture tours.

America: 1882

Aestheticism was sufficiently in vogue to be caricatured by Gilbert and Sullivan in Patience (1881). Richard D'Oyly Carte, an English impresario, invited Wilde to make a lecture tour of North America, simultaneously priming the pump for the US tour of Patience and selling this most charming aesthete to the American public. Wilde journeyed on the SS Arizona, arriving 2 January 1882, and disembarking the following day. Originally planned to last four months, it continued for almost a year due to the commercial success. Wilde sought to transpose the beauty he saw in art into daily life. This was a practical as well as philosophical project: in Oxford he had surrounded himself with blue china and lilies, and now one of his lectures was on interior design.

When asked to explain reports that he had paraded down Piccadilly in London carrying a lily, long hair flowing, Wilde replied, "It's not whether I did it or not that's important, but whether people believed I did it". Wilde believed that the artist should hold forth higher ideals, and that pleasure and beauty would replace utilitarian ethics.

Wilde and aestheticism were both mercilessly caricatured and criticised in the press; the Springfield Republican, for instance, commented on Wilde's behaviour during his visit to Boston to lecture on aestheticism, suggesting that Wilde's conduct was more a bid for notoriety rather than devotion to beauty and the aesthetic. T. W. Higginson, a cleric and abolitionist, wrote in "Unmanly Manhood" of his general concern that Wilde, "whose only distinction is that he has written a thin volume of very mediocre verse", would improperly influence the behaviour of men and women.

According to biographer Michèle Mendelssohn, Wilde was the subject of anti-Irish caricature and was portrayed as a monkey, a blackface performer and a Christy's Minstrel throughout his career. "Harper's Weekly put a sunflower-worshipping monkey dressed as Wilde on the front of the January 1882 issue. The magazine didn't let its reputation for quality impede its expression of what are now considered odious ethnic and racial ideologies. The drawing stimulated other American maligners and, in England, had a full-page reprint in the Lady's Pictorial. ... When the National Republican discussed Wilde, it was to explain 'a few items as to the animal's pedigree.' And on 22 January 1882 the Washington Post illustrated the Wild Man of Borneo alongside Oscar Wilde of England and asked 'How far is it from this to this?' "Though his press reception was hostile, Wilde was well received in diverse settings across America; he drank whiskey with miners in Leadville, Colorado, and was fêted at the most fashionable salons in many cities he visited.

London life and marriage

His earnings, plus expected income from The Duchess of Padua, allowed him to move to Paris between February and mid-May 1883. While there he met Robert Sherard, whom he entertained constantly. "We are dining on the Duchess tonight", Wilde would declare before taking him to an expensive restaurant. In August he briefly returned to New York for the production of Vera, his first play, after it was turned down in London. He reportedly entertained the other passengers with "Ave Imperatrix!, A Poem on England", about the rise and fall of empires. E. C. Stedman, in Victorian Poets, describes this "lyric to England" as "manly verse – a poetic and eloquent invocation". The play was initially well received by the audience, but when the critics wrote lukewarm reviews, attendance fell sharply and the play closed a week after it had opened.

Wilde had to return to England, where he continued to lecture on topics including Personal Impressions of America, The Value of Art in Modern Life, and Dress.

In London, he had been introduced in 1881 to Constance Lloyd, daughter of Horace Lloyd, a wealthy Queen's Counsel, and his wife. She happened to be visiting Dublin in 1884, when Wilde was lecturing at the Gaiety Theatre. He proposed to her, and they married on 29 May 1884 at the Anglican St James's Church, Paddington, in London. Although Constance had an annual allowance of £250, which was generous for a young woman (equivalent to about £25,600 in current value), the Wildes had relatively luxurious tastes. They had preached to others for so long on the subject of design that people expected their home to set new standards. No. 16, Tite Street was duly renovated in seven months at considerable expense. The couple had two sons together, Cyril (1885) and Vyvyan (1886). Wilde became the sole literary signatory of George Bernard Shaw's petition for a pardon of the anarchists arrested (and later executed) after the Haymarket massacre in Chicago in 1886.

Robert Ross had read Wilde's poems before they met at Oxford in 1886. He seemed unrestrained by the Victorian prohibition against homosexuality, and became estranged from his family. By Richard Ellmann's account, he was a precocious seventeen-year-old who "so young and yet so knowing, was determined to seduce Wilde". According to Daniel Mendelsohn, Wilde, who had long alluded to Greek love, was "initiated into homosexual sex" by Ross, while his "marriage had begun to unravel after his wife's second pregnancy, which left him physically repelled".

Prose writing: 1886–91

Journalism and editorship: 1886–89

Criticism over artistic matters in The Pall Mall Gazette provoked a letter in self-defence, and soon Wilde was a contributor to that and other journals during 1885–87. He enjoyed reviewing and journalism; the form suited his style. He could organise and share his views on art, literature and life, yet in a format less tedious than lecturing. Buoyed up, his reviews were largely chatty and positive. Wilde, like his parents before him, also supported the cause of Irish nationalism. When Charles Stewart Parnell was falsely accused of inciting murder, Wilde wrote a series of astute columns defending him in the Daily Chronicle.

His flair, having previously been put mainly into socialising, suited journalism and rapidly attracted notice. With his youth nearly over, and a family to support, in mid-1887 Wilde became the editor of The Lady's World magazine, his name prominently appearing on the cover. He promptly renamed it as The Woman's World and raised its tone, adding serious articles on parenting, culture, and politics, while keeping discussions of fashion and arts. Two pieces of fiction were usually included, one to be read to children, the other for the ladies themselves. Wilde worked hard to solicit good contributions from his wide artistic acquaintance, including those of Lady Wilde and his wife Constance, while his own "Literary and Other Notes" were themselves popular and amusing.

The initial vigour and excitement which he brought to the job began to fade as administration, commuting and office life became tedious. At the same time as Wilde's interest flagged, the publishers became concerned anew about circulation: sales, at the relatively high price of one shilling, remained low. Increasingly sending instructions to the magazine by letter, Wilde began a new period of creative work and his own column appeared less regularly. In October 1889, Wilde had finally found his voice in prose and, at the end of the second volume, Wilde left The Woman's World. The magazine outlasted him by one issue.

If Wilde's period at the helm of the magazine was a mixed success from an organizational point of view, it played a pivotal role in his development as a writer and facilitated his ascent to fame. Whilst Wilde the journalist supplied articles under the guidance of his editors, Wilde the editor was forced to learn to manipulate the literary marketplace on his own terms.

During the late 1880s, Wilde was a close friend of the artist James NcNeill Whistler and they dined together on many occasions. At one of these dinners, Whistler said a bon mot that Wilde found particularly witty, Wilde exclaimed that he wished that he had said it, and Whistler retorted "You will, Oscar, you will". Herbert Vivian—a mutual friend of Wilde and Whistler—attended the dinner and recorded it in his article The Reminiscences of a Short Life which appeared in The Sun in 1889. The article alleged that Wilde had a habit of passing off other people's witticisms as his own—especially Whistler's. Wilde considered Vivian's article to be a scurrilous betrayal, and it directly caused the broken friendship between Wilde and Whistler. The Reminiscences also caused great acrimony between Wilde and Vivian, Wilde accusing Vivian of "the inaccuracy of an eavesdropper with the method of a blackmailer" and banishing Vivian from his circle.

Shorter fiction

Wilde published The Happy Prince and Other Tales in 1888, and had been regularly writing fairy stories for magazines. In 1891 he published two more collections, Lord Arthur Savile's Crime and Other Stories, and in September A House of Pomegranates was dedicated "To Constance Mary Wilde". "The Portrait of Mr. W. H.", which Wilde had begun in 1887, was first published in Blackwood's Edinburgh Magazine in July 1889.It is a short story, which reports a conversation, in which the theory that Shakespeare's sonnets were written out of the poet's love of the boy actor "Willie Hughes", is advanced, retracted, and then propounded again. The only evidence for this is two supposed puns within the sonnets themselves.

The anonymous narrator is at first sceptical, then believing, finally flirtatious with the reader: he concludes that "there is really a great deal to be said of the Willie Hughes theory of Shakespeare's sonnets." By the end fact and fiction have melded together.Arthur Ransome wrote that Wilde "read something of himself into Shakespeare's sonnets" and became fascinated with the "Willie Hughes theory" despite the lack of biographical evidence for the historical William Hughes' existence. Instead of writing a short but serious essay on the question, Wilde tossed the theory amongst the three characters of the story, allowing it to unfold as background to the plot. The story thus is an early masterpiece of Wilde's combining many elements that interested him: conversation, literature and the idea that to shed oneself of an idea one must first convince another of its truth.Ransome concludes that Wilde succeeds precisely because the literary criticism is unveiled with such a deft touch.

Though containing nothing but "special pleading", it would not, he says "be possible to build an airier castle in Spain than this of the imaginary William Hughes" we continue listening nonetheless to be charmed by the telling. "You must believe in Willie Hughes," Wilde told an acquaintance, "I almost do, myself."

Essays and dialogues

Wilde, having tired of journalism, had been busy setting out his aesthetic ideas more fully in a series of longer prose pieces which were published in the

274

major literary-intellectual journals of the day. In January 1889, The Decay of Lying: A Dialogue appeared in The Nineteenth Century, and Pen, Pencil and Poison, a satirical biography of Thomas Griffiths Wainewright, in The Fortnightly Review, edited by Wilde's friend Frank Harris. Two of Wilde's four writings on aesthetics are dialogues: though Wilde had evolved professionally from lecturer to writer, he retained an oral tradition of sorts. Having always excelled as a wit and raconteur, he often composed by assembling phrases, bons mots and witticisms into a longer, cohesive work.

Wilde was concerned about the effect of moralising on art; he believed in art's redemptive, developmental powers: "Art is individualism, and individualism is a disturbing and disintegrating force. There lies its immense value. For what it seeks is to disturb monotony of type, slavery of custom, tyranny of habit, and the reduction of man to the level of a machine." In his only political text, The Soul of Man Under Socialism, he argued political conditions should establish this primacy – private property should be abolished, and cooperation should be substituted for competition. At the same time, he stressed that the government most amenable to artists was no government at all. Wilde envisioned a society where mechanisation has freed human effort from the burden of necessity, effort which can instead be expended on artistic creation. George Orwell summarised, "In effect, the world will be populated by artists, each striving after perfection in the way that seems best to him."

This point of view did not align him with the Fabians, intellectual socialists who advocated using state apparatus to change social conditions, nor did it endear him to the monied classes whom he had previously entertained. Hesketh Pearson, introducing a collection of Wilde's essays in 1950, remarked how The Soul of Man Under Socialism had been an inspirational text for revolutionaries in Tsarist Russia but laments that in the Stalinist era "it is doubtful whether there are any uninspected places in which it could now be hidden".

Wilde considered including this pamphlet and The Portrait of Mr. W.H., his essay-story on Shakespeare's sonnets, in a new anthology in 1891, but eventually decided to limit it to purely aesthetic subjects. Intentions packaged revisions of four essays: The Decay of Lying, Pen, Pencil and Poison, The Truth of Masks (first published 1885), and The Critic as Artist in two parts. For Pearson the biographer, the essays and dialogues exhibit every aspect of Wilde's genius and character: wit, romancer, talker, lecturer, humanist and scholar and concludes that "no other productions of his have as varied an appeal". 1891 turned out to be Wilde's annus mirabilis; apart from his three collections he also produced his only novel.

The Picture of Dorian Gray

The first version of The Picture of Dorian Gray was published as the lead story in the July 1890 edition of Lippincott's Monthly Magazine, along with five others. The story begins with a man painting a picture of Gray. When Gray, who has a "face like ivory and rose leaves", sees his finished portrait, he breaks down. Distraught that his beauty will fade while the portrait stays beautiful, he inadvertently makes a Faustian bargain in which only the painted image grows old while he stays beautiful and young. For Wilde, the purpose of art would be to guide life as if beauty alone were its object. As Gray's portrait allows him to escape the corporeal ravages of his hedonism, Wilde sought to juxtapose the beauty he saw in art with daily life.

Reviewers immediately criticised the novel's decadence and homosexual allusions; The Daily Chronicle for example, called it "unclean", "poisonous", and "heavy with the mephitic odours of moral and spiritual putrefaction". Which he clarified his stance on ethics and aesthetics in art – "If a work of art is rich and vital and complete, those who have artistic instincts will see its beauty and those to whom ethics appeal more strongly will see its moral lesson." He nevertheless revised it extensively for book publication in 1891: six new chapters were added, some overtly decadent passages and homo-eroticism excised, and a preface was included consisting of twenty two epigrams, such as "Books are well written, or badly written. That is all."

Contemporary reviewers and modern critics have postulated numerous possible sources of the story, a search Jershua McCormack argues is futile because Wilde "has tapped a root of Western folklore so deep and ubiquitous that the story has escaped its origins and returned to the oral tradition."Wilde claimed the plot was "an idea that is as old as the history of literature but to which I have given a new form".Modern critic Robin McKie considered the novel to be technically mediocre, saying that the conceit of the plot had guaranteed its fame, but the device is never pushed to its full.On the other hand, Robert McCrum of The Guardian deemed it the 27th best novel ever written in English, calling it "an arresting, and slightly camp, exercise in late-Victorian gothic."

Theatrical career: 1892–95

Salomé

The 1891 census records the Wildes' residence at 16 Tite Street, where he lived with his wife Constance and two sons. Wilde though, not content with being better known than ever in London, returned to Paris in October 1891, this time as a respected writer. He was received at the salons littéraires, including the famous mardis of Stéphane Mallarmé, a renowned symbolist poet of the time. Wilde's two plays during the 1880s, Vera; or, The Nihilists and The Duchess of Padua, had not met with much success. He had continued his interest in the theatre and now, after finding his voice in prose, his thoughts turned again to the dramatic form as the biblical iconography of Salome filled his mind. One evening, after discussing depictions of Salome throughout history, he returned to his hotel and noticed a blank copybook lying on the desk, and it occurred to him to write in it what he had been saying. The result was a new play, Salomé, written rapidly and in French.

A tragedy, it tells the story of Salome, the stepdaughter of the tetrarch Herod Antipas, who, to her stepfather's dismay but mother's delight, requests the head of Jokanaan (John the Baptist) on a silver platter as a reward for dancing the Dance of the Seven Veils. When Wilde returned to London just before Christmas the Paris Echo referred to him as "le great event" of the season. Rehearsals of the play, starring Sarah Bernhardt, began but the play was refused a licence by the Lord Chamberlain, since it depicted biblical characters. Salome was published jointly in Paris and London in 1893, but was not performed until 1896 in Paris, during Wilde's later incarceration.

Comedies of society

Wilde, who had first set out to irritate Victorian society with his dress and talking points, then outrage it with Dorian Gray, his novel of vice hidden beneath art, finally found a way to critique society on its own terms. Lady Windermere's Fan was first performed on 20 February 1892 at St James's Theatre, packed with the cream of society. On the surface a witty comedy, there is subtle subversion underneath: "it concludes with collusive concealment rather than collective disclosure". The audience, like Lady Windermere, are forced to soften harsh social codes in favour of a more nuanced view. The play was enormously popular, touring the country for months, but largely trashed by conservative critics. It was followed by A Woman of No Importance in 1893, another Victorian comedy, revolving around the spectre of illegitimate births, mistaken identities and late revelations. Wilde was commissioned to write two more plays and An Ideal Husband, written in 1894, followed in January 1895.

Peter Raby said these essentially English plays were well-pitched, "Wilde, with one eye on the dramatic genius of Ibsen, and the other on the commercial competition in London's West End, targeted his audience with adroit precision".

Queensberry family

In mid-1891 Lionel Johnson introduced Wilde to Lord Alfred Douglas, Johnson's cousin and an undergraduate at Oxford at the time. Known to his family and friends as "Bosie", he was a handsome and spoilt young man. An intimate friendship sprang up between Wilde and Douglas and by 1893 Wilde was infatuated with Douglas and they consorted together regularly in a tempestuous affair. If Wilde was relatively indiscreet, even flamboyant, in the way he acted, Douglas was reckless in public. Wilde, who was earning up to £100 a week from his plays (his salary at The Woman's World had been £6), indulged Douglas's every whim: material, artistic or sexual.

Douglas soon initiated Wilde into the Victorian underground of gay prostitution and Wilde was introduced to a series of young working-class male prostitutes from 1892 onwards by Alfred Taylor. These infrequent rendezvous usually took the same form: Wilde would meet the boy, offer him gifts, dine him privately and then take him to a hotel room. Unlike Wilde's idealised relations with Ross, John Gray, and Douglas, all of whom remained part of his aesthetic circle, these consorts were uneducated and knew nothing of literature. Soon his public and private lives had become sharply divided; in De Profundis he wrote to Douglas that "It was like feasting with panthers; the danger was half the excitement... I did not know that when they were to strike at me it was to be at another's piping and at another's pay."

Douglas and some Oxford friends founded a journal, The Chameleon, to which Wilde "sent a page of paradoxes originally destined for the Saturday Review". "Phrases and Philosophies for the Use of the Young" was to come under attack six months later at Wilde's trial, where he was forced to defend the magazine to which he had sent his work. In any case, it became unique: The Chameleon was not published again.

Lord Alfred's father, the Marquess of Queensberry, was known for his outspoken atheism, brutish manner and creation of the modern rules of boxing. Queensberry, who feuded regularly with his son, confronted Wilde and Lord Alfred about the nature of their relationship several times, but Wilde was able to mollify him. In June 1894, he called on Wilde at 16 Tite Street, without an appointment, and clarified his stance: "I do not say that you are it, but you look it, and pose at it, which is just as bad. And if I catch you and my son again in any public restaurant I will thrash you" to which Wilde responded: "I don't know what the Queensberry rules are, but the Oscar Wilde rule is to shoot on sight". His account in De Profundis was less triumphant: "It was when, in my library at Tite Street, waving his small hands in the air in epileptic fury, your father... stood uttering every foul word his foul mind could think of, and screaming the loathsome threats he afterwards with such cunning carried out". Queensberry only described the scene once, saying Wilde had "shown him the white feather", meaning he had acted in a cowardly way. Though trying to remain calm, Wilde saw that he was becoming ensnared in a brutal family quarrel. He did not wish to bear Queensberry's insults, but he knew to confront him could lead to disaster were his liaisons disclosed publicly.

The Importance of Being Earnest

Wilde's final play again returns to the theme of switched identities: the play's two protagonists engage in "bunburying" (the maintenance of alternative personas in the town and country) which allows them to escape Victorian social mores.Earnest is even lighter in tone than Wilde's earlier comedies. While their characters often rise to serious themes in moments of crisis, Earnest lacks the by-now stock Wildean characters: there is no "woman with a past", the principals are neither villainous nor cunning, simply idle cultivés, and the idealistic young women are not that innocent. Mostly set in drawing rooms and almost completely lacking in action or violence, Earnest lacks the self-conscious decadence found in The Picture of Dorian Gray and Salome.

The play, now considered Wilde's masterpiece, was rapidly written in Wilde's artistic maturity in late 1894. It was first performed on 14 February 1895, at St James's Theatre in London, Wilde's second collaboration with George Alexander, the actor-manager. Both author and producer assiduously revised, prepared and rehearsed every line, scene and setting in the months before the premiere, creating a carefully constructed representation of late-Victorian society, yet simultaneously mocking it. During rehearsal Alexander requested that Wilde shorten the play from four acts to three, which the author did. Premieres at St James's seemed like "brilliant parties", and the opening of The Importance of Being Earnest was no exception. Allan Aynesworth (who played Algernon) recalled to Hesketh Pearson, "In my fifty-three years of acting, I never remember a greater triumph than [that] first night."Earnest's immediate reception as Wilde's best work to date finally crystallised his fame into a solid artistic reputation. The Importance of Being Earnest remains his most popular play.

Wilde's professional success was mirrored by an escalation in his feud with Queensberry. Queensberry had planned to insult Wilde publicly by throwing a bouquet of rotting vegetables onto the stage; Wilde was tipped off and had Queensberry barred from entering the theatre.Fifteen weeks later Wilde was in prison.

Trials

280

Wilde v. Queensberry

On 18 February 1895, the Marquess left his calling card at Wilde's club, the Albemarle, inscribed: "For Oscar Wilde, posing somdomite" Wilde, encouraged by Douglas and against the advice of his friends, initiated a private prosecution against Queensberry for libel, since the note amounted to a public accusation that Wilde had committed the crime of sodomy.

Queensberry was arrested for criminal libel; a charge carrying a possible sentence of up to two years in prison. Under the 1843 Libel Act, Queensberry could avoid conviction for libel only by demonstrating that his accusation was in fact true, and furthermore that there was some "public benefit" to having made the accusation openly. Queensberry's lawyers thus hired private detectives to find evidence of Wilde's homosexual liaisons.

Wilde's friends had advised him against the prosecution at a Saturday Review meeting at the Café Royal on 24 March 1895; Frank Harris warned him that "they are going to prove sodomy against you" and advised him to flee to France. Wilde and Douglas walked out in a huff, Wilde saying "it is at such moments as these that one sees who are one's true friends". The scene was witnessed by George Bernard Shaw who recalled it to Arthur Ransome a day or so before Ransome's trial for libelling Douglas in 1913. To Ransome it confirmed what he had said in his 1912 book on Wilde; that Douglas's rivalry for Wilde with Robbie Ross and his arguments with his father had resulted in Wilde's public disaster; as Wilde wrote in De Profundis. Douglas lost his case. Shaw included an account of the argument between Harris, Douglas and Wilde in the preface to his play The Dark Lady of the Sonnets.

The libel trial became a cause célèbre as salacious details of Wilde's private life with Taylor and Douglas began to appear in the press. A team of private detectives had directed Queensberry's lawyers, led by Edward Carson QC, to the world of the Victorian underground. Wilde's association with blackmailers and male prostitutes, cross-dressers and homosexual brothels was recorded, and various persons involved were interviewed, some being coerced to appear as witnesses since they too were accomplices to the crimes of which Wilde was accused.

The trial opened on 3 April 1895 before Justice Richard Henn Collins amid scenes of near hysteria both in the press and the public galleries. The extent of the evidence massed against Wilde forced him to declare meekly, "I am the prosecutor in this case"Wilde's lawyer, Sir Edward George Clarke, opened the case by pre-emptively asking Wilde about two suggestive letters Wilde had written to Douglas, which the defence had in its possession. He characterised the first as a "prose sonnet" and admitted that the "poetical language" might seem strange to the court but claimed its intent was innocent. Wilde stated that the letters had been obtained by blackmailers who had attempted to extort money from him, but he had refused, suggesting they should take the £60 (equal to £6,800 today) offered, "unusual for a prose piece of that length". He claimed to regard the letters as works of art rather than something of which to be ashamed.

Carson, a fellow Dubliner who had attended Trinity College, Dublin at the same time as Wilde, cross-examined Wilde on how he perceived the moral content of his works. Wilde replied with characteristic wit and flippancy, claiming that works of art are not capable of being moral or immoral but only well or poorly made, and that only "brutes and illiterates", whose views on art "are incalculably stupid", would make such judgements about art. Carson, a leading barrister, diverged from the normal practice of asking closed questions. Carson pressed Wilde on each topic from every angle, squeezing out nuances of meaning from Wilde's answers, removing them from their aesthetic context and portraying Wilde as evasive and decadent. While Wilde won the most laughs from the court, Carson scored the most legal points. To undermine Wilde's credibility, and to justify Queensberry's description of Wilde as a "posing somdomite", Carson drew from the witness an admission of his capacity for "posing", by demonstrating that he had lied about his age on oath. Playing on this, he returned to the topic throughout his cross-examination. Carson also tried to justify Queensberry's characterisation by quoting from Wilde's novel, The Picture of Dorian Gray, referring in particular to a scene in the second chapter, in which Lord Henry Wotton explains his decadent philosophy to Dorian, an "innocent young man", in Carson's words.

282

Carson then moved to the factual evidence and questioned Wilde about his friendships with younger, lower-class men. Wilde admitted being on a first-name basis and lavishing gifts upon them, but insisted that nothing untoward had occurred and that the men were merely good friends of his. Carson repeatedly pointed out the unusual nature of these relationships and insinuated that the men were prostitutes. Wilde replied that he did not believe in social barriers, and simply enjoyed the society of young men. Then Carson asked Wilde directly whether he had ever kissed a certain servant boy, Wilde responded, "Oh, dear no. He was a particularly plain boy – unfortunately ugly – I pitied him for it." Carson pressed him on the answer, repeatedly asking why the boy's ugliness was relevant. Wilde hesitated, then for the first time became flustered: "You sting me and insult me and try to unnerve me; and at times one says things flippantly when one ought to speak more seriously."

In his opening speech for the defence, Carson announced that he had located several male prostitutes who were to testify that they had had sex with Wilde. On the advice of his lawyers, Wilde dropped the prosecution. Queensberry was found not guilty, as the court declared that his accusation that Wilde was "posing as a Somdomite " was justified, "true in substance and in fact".Under the Libel Act 1843, Queensberry's acquittal rendered Wilde legally liable for the considerable expenses Queensberry had incurred in his defence, which left Wilde bankrupt.

Regina v. Wilde

After Wilde left the court, a warrant for his arrest was applied for on charges of sodomy and gross indecency. Robbie Ross found Wilde at the Cadogan Hotel, Pont Street, Knightsbridge, with Reginald Turner; both men advised Wilde to go at once to Dover and try to get a boat to France; his mother advised him to stay and fight. Wilde, lapsing into inaction, could only say, "The train has gone. It's too late."On 6 April 1895, Wilde was arrested for "gross indecency" under Section 11 of the Criminal Law Amendment Act 1885, a term meaning homosexual acts not amounting to buggery (an offence under a separate statute). At Wilde's instruction, Ross and Wilde's butler forced their way into the bedroom and library of 16 Tite Street, packing some personal effects, manuscripts, and letters. Wilde was then imprisoned on remand at Holloway, where he received daily visits from Douglas.

Events moved quickly and his prosecution opened on 26 April 1895, before Mr Justice Charles. Wilde pleaded not guilty. He had already begged Douglas to leave London for Paris, but Douglas complained bitterly, even wanting to give evidence; he was pressed to go and soon fled to the Hotel du Monde. Fearing persecution, Ross and many others also left the United Kingdom during this time. Under cross examination Wilde was at first hesitant, then spoke eloquently:

Charles Gill (prosecuting): What is "the love that dare not speak its name"?

Wilde: "The love that dare not speak its name" in this century is such a great affection of an elder for a younger man as there was between David and Jonathan, such as Plato made the very basis of his philosophy, and such as you find in the sonnets of Michelangelo and Shakespeare. It is that deep spiritual affection that is as pure as it is perfect. It dictates and pervades great works of art, like those of Shakespeare and Michelangelo, and those two letters of mine, such as they are. It is in this century misunderstood, so much misunderstood that it may be described as "the love that dare not speak its name", and on that account of it I am placed where I am now. It is beautiful, it is fine, it is the noblest form of affection. There is nothing unnatural about it. It is intellectual, and it repeatedly exists between an older and a younger man, when the older man has intellect, and the younger man has all the joy, hope and glamour of life before him. That it should be so, the world does not understand. The world mocks at it, and sometimes puts one in the pillory for it.

This response was counter-productive in a legal sense as it only served to reinforce the charges of homosexual behaviour.

The trial ended with the jury unable to reach a verdict. Wilde's counsel, Sir Edward Clarke, was finally able to get a magistrate to allow Wilde and his friends to post bail. The Reverend Stewart Headlam put up most of the £5,000 surety required by the court, having disagreed with Wilde's treatment by the press and the courts. Wilde was freed from Holloway and, shunning attention, went into hiding at the house of Ernest and Ada Leverson, two of his firm friends. Edward Carson approached Frank Lockwood QC, the Solicitor General and asked "Can we not let up on the fellow now?"Lockwood answered that he would like to do so, but feared that the case had become too politicised to be dropped.

The final trial was presided over by Mr Justice Wills. On 25 May 1895 Wilde and Alfred Taylor were convicted of gross indecency and sentenced to two years' hard labour.The judge described the sentence, the maximum allowed, as "totally inadequate for a case such as this", and that the case was "the worst case I have ever tried". Wilde's response "And I? May I say nothing, my Lord?" was drowned out in cries of "Shame" in the courtroom.

Imprisonment

When first I was put into prison some people advised me to try and forget who I was. It was ruinous advice. It is only by realising what I am that I have found comfort of any kind. Now I am advised by others to try on my release to forget that I have ever been in a prison at all. I know that would be equally fatal. It would mean that I would always be haunted by an intolerable sense of disgrace, and that those things that are meant for me as much as for anybody else – the beauty of the sun and moon, the pageant of the seasons, the music of daybreak and the silence of great nights, the rain falling through the leaves, or the dew creeping over the grass and making it silver – would all be tainted for me, and lose their healing power, and their power of communicating joy. To regret one's own experiences is to arrest one's own development. To deny one's own experiences is to put a lie into the lips of one's own life. It is no less than a denial of the soul.

De Profundis

Wilde was incarcerated from 25 May 1895 to 18 May 1897.

He first entered Newgate Prison in London for processing, then was moved to Pentonville Prison, where the "hard labour" to which he had been sentenced consisted of many hours of walking a treadmill and picking oakum (separating the fibres in scraps of old navy ropes), and where prisoners were allowed to read only the Bible and The Pilgrim's Progress.

A few months later he was moved to Wandsworth Prison in London. Inmates there also followed the regimen of "hard labour, hard fare and a hard bed", which wore harshly on Wilde's delicate health. In November he collapsed during chapel from illness and hunger. His right ear drum was ruptured in the fall, an injury that later contributed to his death. He spent two months in the infirmary.

Richard B. Haldane, the Liberal MP and reformer, visited Wilde and had him transferred in November to Reading Gaol, 30 miles (48 km) west of London on 23 November 1895. The transfer itself was the lowest point of his incarceration, as a crowd jeered and spat at him on the railway platform. He spent the remainder of his sentence there, addressed and identified only as "C33" – the occupant of the third cell on the third floor of C ward.

About five months after Wilde arrived at Reading Gaol, Charles Thomas Wooldridge, a trooper in the Royal Horse Guards, was brought to Reading to await his trial for murdering his wife on 29 March 1896; on 17 June Wooldridge was sentenced to death and returned to Reading for his execution, which took place on Tuesday, 7 July 1896 – the first hanging at Reading in 18 years. From Wooldridge's hanging, Wilde later wrote The Ballad of Reading Gaol.

Wilde was not, at first, even allowed paper and pen but Haldane eventually succeeded in allowing access to books and writing materials. Wilde requested, among others: the Bible in French; Italian and German grammars; some Ancient Greek texts, Dante's Divine Comedy, Joris-Karl Huysmans's new French novel about Christian redemption En route, and essays by St Augustine, Cardinal Newman and Walter Pater.

Between January and March 1897 Wilde wrote a 50,000-word letter to Douglas. He was not allowed to send it, but was permitted to take it with him when released from prison. In reflective mode, Wilde coldly examines his career to date, how he had been a colourful agent provocateur in Victorian society, his art, like his paradoxes, seeking to subvert as well as sparkle. His own estimation of himself was: one who "stood in symbolic relations to the art and culture of my age". It was from these heights that his life with Douglas began, and Wilde examines that particularly closely, repudiating him for what Wilde finally sees as his arrogance and vanity: he had not forgotten Douglas' remark, when he was ill, "When you are not on your pedestal you are not interesting." Wilde blamed himself, though, for the ethical degradation of character that he allowed Douglas to bring about in him and took responsibility for his own fall, "I am here for having tried to put your father in prison." The first half concludes with Wilde forgiving Douglas, for his own sake as much as Douglas's. The second half of the letter traces Wilde's spiritual journey of redemption and fulfilment through his prison reading. He realised that his ordeal had filled his soul with the fruit of experience, however bitter it tasted at the time.

> ... I wanted to eat of the fruit of all the trees in the garden of the world ... And so, indeed, I went out, and so I lived. My only mistake was that I confined myself so exclusively to the trees of what seemed to me the sun-lit side of the garden, and shunned the other side for its shadow and its gloom.

Wilde was released from prison on 19 May 1897 and sailed that evening for Dieppe, France. He never returned to the UK.

On his release, he gave the manuscript to Ross, who may or may not have carried out Wilde's instructions to send a copy to Douglas (who later denied having received it). The letter was partially published in 1905 as De Profundis; its complete and correct publication first occurred in 1962 in The Letters of Oscar Wilde.

Decline: 1897–1900

Exile

Though Wilde's health had suffered greatly from the harshness and diet of prison, he had a feeling of spiritual renewal. He immediately wrote to the Society of Jesus requesting a six-month Catholic retreat; when the request was denied, Wilde wept."I intend to be received into the Catholic Church before long", Wilde told a journalist who asked about his religious intentions.

He spent his last three years impoverished and in exile. He took the name "Sebastian Melmoth", after Saint Sebastian and the titular character of Melmoth the Wanderer (a Gothic novel by Charles Maturin, Wilde's great-uncle).Wilde wrote two long letters to the editor of the Daily Chronicle, describing the brutal conditions of English prisons and advocating penal reform. His discussion of the dismissal of Warder Martin for giving biscuits to an anaemic child prisoner repeated the themes of the corruption and degeneration of punishment that he had earlier outlined in The Soul of Man under Socialism.

Wilde spent mid-1897 with Robert Ross in the seaside village of Berneval-le-Grand in northern France, where he wrote The Ballad of Reading Gaol, narrating the execution of Charles Thomas Wooldridge, who murdered his wife in a rage at her infidelity. It moves from an objective story-telling to symbolic identification with the prisoners. No attempt is made to assess the justice of the laws which convicted them but rather the poem highlights the brutalisation of the punishment that all convicts share. Wilde juxtaposes the executed man and himself with the line "Yet each man kills the thing he loves". He adopted the proletarian ballad form and the author was credited as "C33", Wilde's cell number in Reading Gaol. He suggested that it be published in Reynolds' Magazine, "because it circulates widely among the criminal classes – to which I now belong – for once I will be read by my peers – a new experience for me". It was an immediate roaring commercial success, going through seven editions in less than two years, only after which "[Oscar" was added to the title page, though many in literary circles had known Wilde to be the author. It brought him a small amount of money.

Although Douglas had been the cause of his misfortunes, he and Wilde were reunited in August 1897 at Rouen. This meeting was disapproved of by the friends and families of both men. Constance Wilde was already refusing to meet Wilde or allow him to see their sons, though she sent him money – three pounds a week. During the latter part of 1897, Wilde and Douglas lived together near Naples for a few months until they were separated by their families under the threat of cutting off all funds.

Wilde's final address was at the dingy Hôtel d'Alsace (now known as L'Hôtel), on rue des Beaux-Arts in Saint-Germain-des-Prés, Paris. "This poverty really breaks one's heart: it is so sale , so utterly depressing, so hopeless. Pray do what you can" he wrote to his publisher.He corrected and published An Ideal Husband and The Importance of Being Earnest, the proofs of which, according to Ellmann, show a man "very much in command of himself and of the play" but he refused to write anything else: "I can write, but have lost the joy of writing".

He wandered the boulevards alone and spent what little money he had on alcohol. A series of embarrassing chance encounters with hostile English visitors, or Frenchmen he had known in better days, drowned his spirit. Soon Wilde was sufficiently confined to his hotel to joke, on one of his final trips outside, "My wallpaper and I are fighting a duel to the death. One of us has got to go". On 12 October 1900 he sent a telegram to Ross: "Terribly weak. Please come". His moods fluctuated; Max Beerbohm relates how their mutual friend Reginald 'Reggie' Turner had found Wilde very depressed after a nightmare. "I dreamt that I had died, and was supping with the dead!" "I am sure", Turner replied, "that you must have been the life and soul of the party."Turner was one of the few of the old circle who remained with Wilde to the end and was at his bedside when he died.

Death

By 25 November 1900 Wilde had developed meningitis, then called "cerebral meningitis". Robbie Ross arrived on 29 November, sent for a priest, and Wilde was conditionally baptised into the Catholic Church by Fr Cuthbert Dunne, a Passionist priest from Dublin,Wilde having been baptised in the Church of Ireland and having moreover a recollection of Catholic baptism as a child, a fact later attested to by the minister of the sacrament, Fr Lawrence Fox.Fr Dunne recorded the baptism,

> As the voiture rolled through the dark streets that wintry night, the sad story of Oscar Wilde was in part repeated to me... Robert Ross knelt by the bedside, assisting me as best he could while I administered conditional baptism, and afterwards answering the responses while I

gave Extreme Unction to the prostrate man and recited the prayers for the dying. As the man was in a semi-comatose condition, I did not venture to administer the Holy Viaticum; still I must add that he could be roused and was roused from this state in my presence. When roused, he gave signs of being inwardly conscious... Indeed I was fully satisfied that he understood me when told that I was about to receive him into the Catholic Church and gave him the Last Sacraments... And when I repeated close to his ear the Holy Names, the Acts of Contrition, Faith, Hope and Charity, with acts of humble resignation to the Will of God, he tried all through to say the words after me.

Wilde died of meningitis on 30 November 1900.Different opinions are given as to the cause of the disease: Richard Ellmann claimed it was syphilitic; Merlin Holland, Wilde's grandson, thought this to be a misconception, noting that Wilde's meningitis followed a surgical intervention, perhaps a mastoidectomy; Wilde's physicians, Dr Paul Cleiss and A'Court Tucker, reported that the condition stemmed from an old suppuration of the right ear (from the prison injury, see above) treated for several years (une ancienne suppuration de l'oreille droite d'ailleurs en traitement depuis plusieurs années) and made no allusion to syphilis.

Burial

Wilde was initially buried in the Cimetière de Bagneux outside Paris; in 1909 his remains were disinterred and transferred to Père Lachaise Cemetery, inside the city. His tomb there was designed by Sir Jacob Epstein. It was commissioned by Robert Ross, who asked for a small compartment to be made for his own ashes, which were duly transferred in 1950. The modernist angel depicted as a relief on the tomb was originally complete with male genitalia, which were initially censored by French Authorities with a golden leaf. The genitals have since been vandalised; their current whereabouts are unknown. In 2000, Leon Johnson, a multimedia artist, installed a silver prosthesis to replace them.In 2011, the tomb was cleaned of the many lipstick marks left there by admirers and a glass barrier was installed to prevent further marks or damage.

The epitaph is a verse from The Ballad of Reading Gaol,

And alien tears will fill for him

Pity's long-broken urn,

For his mourners will be outcast men,

And outcasts always mourn.

Posthumous pardon

In 2017, Wilde was among an estimated 50,000 men who were pardoned for homosexual acts that were no longer considered offences under the Policing and Crime Act 2017. The Act is known informally as the Alan Turing law.

Honours

In 2014 Wilde was one of the inaugural honorees in the Rainbow Honor Walk, a walk of fame in San Francisco's Castro neighbourhood noting LGBTQ people who have "made significant contributions in their fields."

Biographies

Wilde's life has been the subject of numerous biographies since his death. The earliest were memoirs by those who knew him: often they are personal or impressionistic accounts which can be good character sketches, but are sometimes factually unreliable. Frank Harris, his friend and editor, wrote a biography, Oscar Wilde: His Life and Confessions (1916); though prone to exaggeration and sometimes factually inaccurate, it offers a good literary portrait of Wilde. Lord Alfred Douglas wrote two books about his relationship with Wilde. Oscar Wilde and Myself (1914), largely ghost-written by T. W. H. Crosland, vindictively reacted to Douglas's discovery that De Profundis was addressed to him and defensively tried to distance him from Wilde's scandalous reputation. Both authors later regretted their work. Later, in Oscar Wilde: A Summing Up (1939) and his Autobiography he was more sympathetic to Wilde. Of Wilde's other close friends, Robert Sherard; Robert Ross, his literary executor; and Charles Ricketts variously published biographies, reminiscences or correspondence. The first more or less objective biography of Wilde came about when Hesketh Pearson wrote Oscar Wilde: His Life and Wit (1946). In 1954 Wilde's son Vyvyan Holland published his memoir Son of Oscar Wilde, which recounts the difficulties Wilde's wife and children faced after his imprisonment. It was revised and updated by Merlin Holland in 1989.

Oscar Wilde, a critical study by Arthur Ransome was published in 1912. The book only briefly mentioned Wilde's life, but subsequently Ransome (and The Times Book Club) were sued for libel by Lord Alfred Douglas. In April 1913 Douglas lost the libel action after a reading of De Profundis refuted his claims.

Richard Ellmann wrote his 1987 biography Oscar Wilde, for which he posthumously won a National (USA) Book Critics Circle Award in 1988and a Pulitzer Prize in 1989. The book was the basis for the 1997 film Wilde, directed by Brian Gilbert and starring Stephen Fry as the title character.

Neil McKenna's 2003 biography, The Secret Life of Oscar Wilde, offers an exploration of Wilde's sexuality. Often speculative in nature, it was widely criticised for its pure conjecture and lack of scholarly rigour. Thomas Wright's Oscar's Books (2008) explores Wilde's reading from his childhood in Dublin to his death in Paris. After tracking down many books that once belonged to Wilde's Tite Street library (dispersed at the time of his trials), Wright was the first to examine Wilde's marginalia.

> Later on, I think everyone will recognise his achievements; his plays and essays will endure. Of course, you may think with others that his personality and conversation were far more wonderful than anything he wrote, so that his written works give only a pale reflection of his power. Perhaps that is so, and of course, it will be impossible to reproduce what is gone forever.

Robert Ross, 23 December 1900

In 2018, Matthew Sturgis' "Oscar: A Life," was published in London. The book incorporates rediscovered letters and other documents and is the most extensively researched biography of Wilde to appear since 1988.

Parisian literati, also produced several biographies and monographs on him. André Gide wrote In Memoriam, Oscar Wilde and Wilde also features in his journals. Thomas Louis, who had earlier translated books on Wilde into French, produced his own L'esprit d'Oscar Wilde in 1920. Modern books include Philippe Jullian's Oscar Wilde, and L'affaire Oscar Wilde, ou, Du danger de laisser la justice mettre le nez dans nos draps (The Oscar Wilde Affair, or, On the Danger of Allowing Justice to put its Nose in our Sheets) by Odon Vallet, a French religious historian. (Source: Wikipedia)

NOTABLE WORKS

ESSAYS

"The Decay of Lying" First published in Nineteenth Century (1889), republished in Intentions (1891).

"Pen, Pencil and Poison" First published in the Fortnightly Review (1889), republished in Intentions (1891).

"The Soul of Man under Socialism" First published in the Fortnightly Review (1891), republished in The Soul of Man (1895), privately printed.

Intentions (1891) Wilde revised his dialogues on aesthetic subjects for publication in this volume, which comprises:

- "The Critic as Artist"
- "The Decay of Lying"
- "Pen, Pencil and Poison"
- "The Truth of Masks"

"Phrases and Philosophies for the Use of the Young" first published in the Oxford student magazine The Chameleon, December 1894)

"A Few Maxims For The Instruction Of The Over-Educated" First published, anonymously, in the 1894 November 17 issue of Saturday Review.

FICTION

Novel

The Picture of Dorian Gray (1890/1891). The first version of "The Picture of Dorian Gray" was published, in a form highly edited by the magazine, as the lead story in the July 1890 edition of Lippincott's Monthly Magazine. Wilde published the longer and revised version in book form in 1891, with an added preface.

Stories

"The Portrait of Mr. W. H." (1889)

The Happy Prince and Other Tales (1888, a collection of fairy tales) consisting of:

- "The Happy Prince"

- "The Nightingale and the Rose"

- "The Selfish Giant"

- "The Devoted Friend"

- "The Remarkable Rocket"

A House of Pomegranates (1891, fairy tales)

Lord Arthur Savile's Crime and Other Stories (1891) Including "The Canterville Ghost" first published in periodical form in 1887.

Complete Short Fiction. Penguin Classics, 2003. Edited with an Introduction and Notes by Ian Small. Contains all works listed above plus Poems in Prose (1894) and one very short 'Elder-tree' (fragment).

POEMS

Ravenna (1878) Winner of the Newdigate Prize.

Poems (1881) Wilde's collection of poetry and first publication.

The Sphinx (1894)

Poems in Prose (1894)

The Ballad of Reading Gaol (1898)

PLAYS

Vera; or, The Nihilists (1880)

The Duchess of Padua (1883)

Lady Windermere's Fan (1892)

A Woman of No Importance (1893)

Salomé (French version) (1893, first performed in Paris 1896)

Salomé: A Tragedy in One Act: Translated from the French of Oscar Wilde by Lord Alfred Douglas, illustrated by Aubrey Beardsley (1894)

An Ideal Husband (1895) (text)

The Importance of Being Earnest (1895) (text)

La Sainte Courtisane and A Florentine Tragedy Fragmentary. First published 1908 in Methuen's Collected Works

(Dates are dates of first performance, which approximate better to the probable date of composition than dates of publication.)

The Importance of Being Earnest and Other Plays. Penguin Classics, 2000. Edited with an Introduction, Commentaries and Notes by Richard Allen Cave. Contains all from above save the first two. Salome is in English.

As an appendix there is one excised scene from The Importance of Being Earnest.

De Profundis (Written 1895-97, in Reading Gaol). Expurgated edition published 1905; suppressed portions 1913, expanded version in The Letters of Oscar Wilde (1962).

The Rise of Historical Criticism (Written while at college) First published in 1905 (Sherwood Press, Hartford, CT) privately printed. Reprinted in Miscellanies, the last volume of the First Collected Edition (1908).

The First Collected Edition (Methuen & Co., 14 volumes) appeared in 1908 and contained many previously unpublished works.

The Second Collected Edition (Methuen & Co., 12 volumes) appeared in installments between 1909–11 and contained several other unpublished works.

The Letters of Oscar Wilde (Written 1868-1900) Published in 1962. Republished as The Complete Letters of Oscar Wilde (2000), with letters discovered since 1962, and new annotations by Merlin Holland.

The Women of Homer (Written 1876, while at college). First published in Oscar Wilde: The Women of Homer (2008) by The Oscar Wilde Society.

The Philosophy of Dress First published in The New-York Tribune (1885), published for the first time in book form in Oscar Wilde On Dress (2013).

MISATTRIBUTED

Teleny, or The Reverse of the Medal (Paris, 1893) has been attributed to Wilde, but its authorship is unclear. One theory is that it was a combined effort by several of Wilde's friends, which he may have edited.

Constance On September 14, 2011, Wilde's grandson Merlin Holland contested Wilde's claimed authorship of this play entitled Constance, scheduled to open that week in the King's Head Theatre. It was not, in fact, "Oscar Wilde's final play," as its producers were claiming. Holland said Wilde did sketch out the play's scenario in 1894, but "never wrote a word" of it, and that "it is dishonest to foist this on the public." The Artistic Director Adam Spreadbury-Maher of the King's Head Theatre and producer of Constance pointed out that Wilde's son, Vyvyan Holland, wrote in 1954, "a significant amount of the dialogue (of Constance) bears the authentic stamp of my father's hand". There is further proof that the developed scenario that Constance was reconstituted from was written by Wilde between 1897 and his death in 1900, rather than the 1894 George Alexander scenario which Merlin Holland quotes.

9 789390 228652